Oliver Grey

A Virgin Widow

Vol. I

Oliver Grey

A Virgin Widow
Vol. I

ISBN/EAN: 9783337046866

Printed in Europe, USA, Canada, Australia, Japan

Cover: Foto ©Andreas Hilbeck / pixelio.de

More available books at **www.hansebooks.com**

BY

OLIVER GREY.

VOL. I.

IN THREE VOLUMES.

London

REMINGTON & CO., PUBLISHERS

HENRIETTA STREET, COVENT GARDEN, W.C.

1886.

TO

E. M. E.

THESE PAGES,

WHICH MAY SERVE TO RECALL SOME

EARLY AND HAPPY HOURS,

ARE

AFFECTIONATELY INSCRIBED.

CONTENTS.

—•—

CHAPTER I

CHAPTER VII.

CHAPTER VIII.

CHAPTER IX.

CHAPTER X.

CHAPTER XI.

CHAPTER XII.

(To be continued.)

A VIRGIN WIDOW.

CHAPTER I.

INTRODUCTORY.

READER,—Have you amongst your circle
of acquaintance, that which is generally
understood to represent a " True Friend,"
one who has grown up with, and is, as it
were, a part of you; a friendship that
quickened in youth, leavened with the
dearest and·happiest associations of your
early life, and is still nearer and dearer to
you; which time has cemented more closely,

a disinterested love, well defined, peculiar
in itself for the absence of any motive ;
a friendship growing apace, more and more
serene and lasting ?   I pause,—the word
last written gives peculiar force to the
meaning, and perhaps will convey to your
mind infinitely more than anything I can
herein describe.   Lasting !—yes !   " Firm
as a rock ! ! "—we will leave it there with
two notes of admiration, and, as it were,
with bayonets fixed, keeping guard over the
words.   Let these our watchwords be.

Have you such a friend ?   Could you
put your hand upon one, amongst your
numerous acquaintances, without the least
doubt or difficulty ?   Can you walk leisurely
amidst a throng of friends (so called by
courtesy, and otherwise), and feel a magnetic influence steal over you, and your
heart beat with a true and lively feeling
for one out of the number ?   If so, bear

with me, whilst, in the most unostentatious
way, I take you, from chapter to chapter,
through this narrative. We shall not journey in these pages as " intimate friends,"
but, I trust, and have the vanity to hope
and believe, that we shall be better friends
long before I close this story; under any
circumstances, I will, with your permission,
take such for granted, and start *de novo* as
" Novel Friends ! "

"Lasting ! "—how one ignores the fact
that, in the very best and happiest sense
of the word, it is but fleeting : to-day, here
is friendship, side by side, in great variety,
confiding, full of love, hope, charity, and
sympathy, imparting pleasure, and sharing
grief : to-morrow, it is cut down by the
certain, restless scythe, that, in its onward
course, sweeps all before it into vast eter-
nity, and, like the green wheat-stalks that
daily thrive under the agriculturalist's care-

ful manipulation, warmed by the penetrating rays of the summer sun, moistened with the dew-breath of heaven, ripen, bear their increase, and yield in turn to the season that asks them to surrender,—so with everything this side of the grave !

"True friend !" Of whom do I speak, and well may it be asked, who represents the personal pronoun ? At this juncture I must pause for a moment, to solicit the indulgence of my critics, in a matter which requires a little explanation.

When first commencing this narrative, it was my intention to write it as an imaginary autobiography ; but, finding the construction in that form difficult to maintain in its entirety (insomuch as many characters had to be introduced), I departed from the fixed rule, using the personal pronoun, and occasionally writing in the third person, when chronicling surrounding events. I therefore trust that my critics (who are ever ready to deal gently with those who have the moral courage to admit a defect) will accord me their forbearance.

" True friend ! "—and *apropos* of the pronoun " I "—the first question is very easily answered ; but to follow it up, in the delineation of the virtues of the fair-haired stripling of whom I have the pleasure and privilege of speaking, is a task which I feel almost incapable of performing. But, in my anxiety to portray a correct reflex of my lamented friend's excellent qualities, I fall short, and stumble over the only tribute I can offer to his memory.

The second question can be answered by this deponent offhand, without hesitation, or, using a well-hackneyed, homely phrase, " beating about the bush," for I am what I am ; and I have a horror of appearing, in the eyes of people, what I am not. Therefore, as my journey with you, courteous reader, will, I trust, be a fairly long one, shut up together, so to speak, in the coach for a considerable time, whilst the wheels fly round, and the boxes occasionally get hot for the want of more oil, or the curb from the leader's bit should be lost on the way, I must claim your indulgence over the rough macadamised road that we shall have to traverse.

First, I am the son of a lord,—yes, a live lord!—but I hasten to qualify that observation by saying, the only claim my father had to such a distinguished title, rests on the silly appellation given to him by still more silly Manchester men, who dubbed him a "Cotton Lord," in consequence of his enormous dealings in that description of merchandise; so I reduce myself at once to the "Commoners," take my name out of the book of "*Who's Who?*" and jot myself down plain Oliver Grey, or, in other words, as some of my facetious subalterns at mess were pleased occasionally to designate me, " the noble and gallant captain ! "

I said my father was called a " Cotton Lord ; " be it observed that the sobriquet was most offensive to him. I well remember, on one occasion, when extravagance brought the contents of my purse to extreme low-water mark, and necessitated my appealing to his generosity, in the hope of having it replenished, I stupidly but jocosely referred, in some playful way, to the obnoxious title, just as he was " finishing " an extraordinary flourish of his, which was invariably the conclusion of his signature to all cheques, when he calmly looked into my face, surveyed me from head to foot, shrugged his shoulders, arched his eyebrows, and deliberately tore the bilious-looking strip of stamped paper into small pieces, throwing them into the waste basket. Although he did not actually use the words, " Call again to-morrow," his dark, flashing eyes told me how offensive my allusion to the " Cotton Lord " was,—which allusion cost me, at least, two hundred bright sovereigns, and taught me a practical lesson, which I have never forgotten. Thinking that his high dudgeon was ephemeral, I did call again on the morrow, but found my father as "firm as a rock," and therefore had to wait, with an empty purse, for the coming round of my next quarterly allowance—about the most humiliating and unpleasant financial process I ever remember to have scrambled through in my early days.

Whilst I am writing a history of some portion of my life, and introducing other persons with whom I have been intimately associated, also making, *en passant*, a cursory reference to numerous odd people I have encountered, I may perhaps be excused, on the score of running too near the danger signal of egotism, from entering into, or venturing upon, very minute details as regards myself, leaving one's actions, which not unfrequently speak unutterable things, to be the best test of true friendship.

Should I be permitted in these pages to feebly discharge obligations I owe, and produce some faithful portraits of loving friends, exhibiting their reflex as nearly as an unpractised brush can portray on the canvas, the finishing touch—soft tints and fine lines, —I will leave to be filled in by an abler and better painter than myself, or, in other words, to the imagination of the reader, who will doubtless gather up the flowers as they are strewn, so to speak, broadcast over these pages, and, may be, enjoy their fragrance in some idle moments. There will, however, as a common result of all the workings and ramifications in the history of this troubled life, be found here and there, from bud to bloom, cultivated flowers, wild flowers, briars, and a conglomeration of entanglements. Various pleasures and griefs, too, are bound up in this volume ; a medley of facts and fiction are also recorded herein, but the whole being thoroughly leavened with fiction, it is as well that my indulgent readers may not be able with certainty to discriminate between counterfeit and real.

I will pass over my early life—those joyous, bright, and never-to-be-forgotten days of youth, the wild-oats season, college experience, graduating, and all that sort of thing —and plunge at once into the battle of life, that bleak wilderness of ours, with all its surroundings and blandishments.

When I attained my twenty-second birthday, I was a subaltern in the —th Regiment, in which I subsequently saw some active service in the Crimean War, was present and took part in the storming of ——, also at the carrying of ——, where I was twice wounded, and had two horses shot under me, for which service I received a medal, clasp, and my captaincy, a gaping sabre wound in the fleshy part of my sword arm, ditto, the result of a gun-shot, which ploughed up an inch or two of the dexter side of my breast, and lastly, from a stamp of my charger's shoe, as a remembrance of the red roan, or his mark, preparatory to his receiving the *coup de grâce* from a round-shot which hailed from the Russian battery. So much for the early part of the campaign,—my dangers, achievements, and laurels various !

A spell of three weeks' comparatively easy work, a general brushing up and restoration of my glorious men, who had hitherto earned for themselves considerable distinction, bring

me to the memorable night of the —th
before ——.

Those who are left, alas! how few of my
brave fellows, that band of highly-tempered
steel and perfection of training under canvas,
and, be it recorded, under fire, will remember with pride and sadness, the men who led
them into the very jaws of the cannon that
belched forth its torrents of destruction, making many wives widows, children fatherless,
and parents childless. Good God! how they
withered! cut into shreds, so to speak, like
the grass before the scythe ; again and again
to the attack, noble fellows! " Onward " was
our watchword ; but the last grand charge!
—that cheer!—those empty saddles!—that
reckless stampede of the enemy, like chaff
before the wind! That sudden wrench, and
the leap into the trenches, where Nelson,
my charger, with his side riddled like a
cullendar with bullets, took his final, fatal

jump, negotiating an earthwork, quite his height, and landing on the top of his grave!

"Where he died like a warrior brave."

When I first obtained my commission in the —th, the *Gazette* of that week contained the announcement of Percival Snowden's appointment to the same regiment, and, in due course, we met officially (though not by any means for the first time) in the mess-room of —— Barracks, full of youth, vigour, life, spirits, and hope. He was an Eton boy; I was an Oxford one. We had been competitors on the river, and also in gymnasium; and verily he was an ugly "customer" at anything when biceps and endurance played a prominent part. He could fairly well hold his own, too, against all comers either at single-stick, boxing, rackets, cricket, and other pastime; his massive head, muscular development, width of chest, healthy complexion, lofty forehead, expressive eyes, and the cut of a determined lip, were sure indications of the life he was peculiarly fitted and trained for, and which he so nobly followed, until cruel fate separated us.

Let me take you back, friendly reader, to the camping-ground, and into our tent on the slopes of ——, within sight of the Russian battery and strong earthwork entrenchments, on the night preceding the memorable —th, and there introduce you to my subaltern, the boy I loved! I dubbed him " boy," as he playfully styled me,—it was our habit to address each other as " my dear old boy," ignoring altogether the absurd epithet!

Chance, and a spice of good luck, once enabled me to render some valuable service in the midst of a scrambling fray with the enemy. When the saddle of General ——'s aide-de-camp was emptied, I took the poor fellow's place, and contrived, after cutting my way through the Russian lines, to convey the general's orders to a battery of Royal Horse Artillery, in (it was said) an incredibly short time, for which piece of luck I was promoted. I name this little coincidence, as fortune only placed me a " peg " higher in rank than my friend, whom I always considered an abler and better soldier than myself.

It was a glorious night, that —th, as we sat round the camp fire, wrapped in our great-coats. We were most of us full of hope and spirits, telling long tales of past stirring events, home scenes, and the merry maids of England. But there were ugly gaps in our ranks; the dark mantle of war had left its sure and certain mark; the stentorian voice of our lamented and gallant captain, that once filled the whole camp with merry sounds, was not to be heard,—it was silenced for ever in this world,—he is " slumbering on earth's cold pillow," with "his martial cloak thrown o'er him," and the pale-faced moon shining over his grave.

"I saw that soldier fall, and the tear that dimmed his eye."

The flames from our camp fire shot up high into the air, and crackled fiercely, casting their lurid light on the surrounding scene, verily a motley group, smoking their meer-schaums, and staring vacantly into the burning embers, imagination conjuring up endless battle scenes, castles, forests, homes, sweethearts, and wives !

"Captain," said Percy, "sing us once more that song you composed."

"I am not much in a singing humour, my dear fellow," I replied, pulling away at my well-coloured pipe, with great emphasis.

"Come old boy, I know you will, if only to oblige me, particularly, after my setting the words to music for you," said Percy.

"I will to-morrow."

"To-morrow! why it may never come, Oliver, to either of us, at least in this world; you may be knocked completely out of tune, and I may be out of time, and perhaps out of—"

He paused. It was a long, dismal, unsatisfactory pause, and suggestive of many interpretations. I took his hand beneath my military cloak, pressed it, and gently whispered,—

"Never, Percy, never! brave, noble fellow! As long as I have a mind to call mine own, your memory will be revered, if that is what you were alluding to."

Percy threw up his large, blue eyes full into my face. I perceived by the light of the flame as it shot up from our camp fire, that they were suffused with tears; and I also observed, for the first time during the campaign, a certain amount of depression in his spirits; his attention appeared much divided; and during our colloquy on several matters relating to the war, his answers to my queries were remarkable for the absence of that enthusiasm which invariably shone out so brightly in his usual temperament, lighting up and cheering the whole camp, at times when success was not quite our portion.

" What is the matter with you to-night, old boy ? " I said, slapping him on the shoulder.

" Nothing—why ? " dismally.

" Well, it occurred to me for the moment, that you had lately received a large legacy, and did not know what to do with it," jocosely.

" I wish I had," said Percy, stretching his hands above his head, and clenching his fists, —a peculiar habit he had whenever anything closely touched his heart.

" Why ? " I replied, my curiosity being excited.

"Because I should, without the least hesitation, find a good use for it," said Percy.

"Exactly; 20 to 4 on Valentine for the Derby," I suggested playfully.

"No!" said Percy, vehemently. "No, Oliver, nothing of the sort. It is my wish, before I leave this world, to do one good act in my life that will benefit—"

"Others, of course," I interrupted, knowing too well that his whole life hitherto had been devoted to everyone but himself.

"Yes," continued Percy, leisurely refilling his pipe, "if only but one small drop in the stream, it will help to turn the mill."

"What is your fancy this time, Percy?"

"A donation to the widows of those brave fellows, who were so unmercifully sliced up in that horrible trench I so recklessly led them."

"You have, however," I replied, "the satisfaction of knowing that, notwithstanding positive orders, your fluke turned out to be of inestimable value, and your promotion will be as certain as—"

" Come, come ; your song, Oliver, your song," interrupted Percy. " I should like to hear it once more before I—"

" The Captain's song," from twenty voices.

As I composed most of my songs, which were set to music by Percy, and our intelligent bandmaster, they always created unusual interest in our camp, and I soon had many scores of brave fellows to listen. It was said, too, that I had a fine voice, which, however, did not quite accord with my beloved mother's notion of her youngest son's vocal powers. She always considered my rendering of songs more like a " bee in a pitcher " than anything else. I have a shrewd suspicion she was right. Be it so ; nevertheless, let the bee hum.

BIRDS OF PREY.

Uprouse, ye sons of old England!
  Keep a watchful and sharp look-out;
Eagles are soaring above us,
  And vultures are flying about.

Awake, then, ye sons of Old England!
  Britannia's dear brothers of steel,
Let your swords fly out of their scabbards,
  Let us give them a jolly good meal.

Uprouse, then, ye boys of Old England!
  Let the lion's loud roaring be heard,
The wag of whose tail I'm sure cannot fail
  To scare such a treacherous bird.

Uprouse, ye good fathers of England!
  Who have wives and dear daughters at home,
Just clip both the wings of these vampires,
  And skin them all clean to the bone.

Uprouse, "one and all" of fair England!
  Let the voice of your rifles be heard;
Leave not a feather of plumage
  On the wings of the ghastly old bird.

"Bravo! bravo! encore, encore," from a hundred voices.

Pipes are refilled, and, it is needless to add, I repeated my song.

"Now Percy, my lad," I said, "strike up, none of your dismals if you please; let us have one of yours; come, 'Sound the Trumpet boldly.'"

"I need no pressing, Oliver, particularly as I have a presentiment it will be the last I shall ever sing."

Those words, uttered in a measured, decided voice, fell upon a score of ears like a funeral knell, and vibrated with intense and painful sensation through our hearts, for we all loved the brave fellow, yea verily! from the drummer to the colonel.

"Come, come, Percy, you are dry, lad, you are dry," I exclaimed, handing him my brandy-flask; "pull at this; a long pull and a strong pull, drink to our sweethearts and—"

"Wives," eagerly interrupted Percy,

seizing the flask, and half finishing its contents.

Shall I ever forget the look he gave me, or the last song the dear fellow sang?— Never!

As the concluding words fell from my brave comrade's lips, the bugle sounded. We knocked out the contents of our pipes, and turned into our tents, with anxious thoughts for the morrow.

CHAPTER II.

STIRRING EVENTS.

"Those sounds that bid the life-blood start,
  Swift to the mantling cheek and beating heart,
  The clang of echoing steel, the charger's neigh,
  The measured tread of hosts in war's array.
  And oh! that music, whose exulting breath,
  Speaks but of glory on the road to death."
                                        Mrs Hemans.

SOMEHOW, I could not sleep for more than an hour together, and whenever I awoke, I quietly took a peep at Percy,—the small glimmering pendant lamp swinging from the top of our tent threw its dismal light on the features of my friend. His bright eyes seemed to me brighter than usual. He smiled, apostrophised a few words, drew a locket from under his waistcoat, which he opened and kissed repeatedly. I knew all about it: it was "the same old story told again," though, this time, at two o'clock in the morning. I knew whose reflex he treasured up next his heart in that circle of gold. Many a pipe had been smoked over that portrait; doubts and difficulties solved, hopes enlivened, and fears scattered, by the soothing influence of the narcotic contents of our black meerschaums, which always had a potent charm for allaying grief.

I say I knew all about it; at least, I thought I did. Percy invariably came to me for advice, and made me his confidant. In like manner I looked towards him, whose heart I knew to be the casket of those little secrets I had to impart, which, I must confess, were but few, and at the most, extended to my father, mother, and financial matters. As for loving any girl, other than my sister, such never entered my head; besides, I was not altogether the most presentable fellow in the county. My father declared that, in the presence of the fair sex, I was surly, ill-conditioned, clumsy, and, I believe, he went once so far as to say, thick-headed boy in creation. He used also to observe—and I never doubted for a moment his veracity,—"Give Oliver his fishing-rod, two ounces of bird's-eye and cavendish mixed, a bottle of milk, and his mother's blessing, and all his wants are supplied;"—barring the milk, which was jocosely included in the quartett of sundry enjoyments, every word was gospel.

That I was my own dear mother's "broth of a boy" I admit, and that she—Heaven bless her!—was my "all in all," are the brightest, happiest, and most comforting recollections of my past life. Her good advice was my daily support; her pattern and the valuable precedents she established in my young mind, have been mighty bulwarks—bulwarks that have proved impervious to the raking shot and shell that are sometimes recklessly hurled by designing men at our frail natures; a mainstay in the hour of peril, a guiding-star in the camp, my shield and buckler under a galling fire, and— I digress.

> How apt one is on loving themes to dwell;
> The mind will wander where we cannot tell!
> Take wings and fly from here to there,
> And bask in other atmosphere.

I again feigned sleep; now and then watching poor Percy, as he restlessly tossed himself from side to side on his camp bed; at times I thought I could discern, by the flickering lamp that was almost extinguished, a bright crimson flush on either side of his face. I was uneasy, feeling that these were symptoms of an approaching fever, which accounted for his extraordinary manner and absence of mind during the last few hours. I revolved it all silently in my mind, as I lay rolled in the blankets, inwardly hoping that he might fall into a sound sleep, which I knew would do more towards restoring him than anything else. His mind was, manifestly, much disturbed, indeed, it had not been tranquil for some time, and my experience in such matters, led me to believe he was about to succumb to a malignant fever, that was just then raging with great intensity in different parts of the camp. An interval of half-an-hour elapsed, during which time, not a sound fell upon my ear, other than the snoring of our comrades; the steady step of the sentinel, as he tramped up and down the well-trodden path; the watchward given to the relief; and the neighing of the picketed horses.

At last, finding that sleep had entirely for

saken me, and that the pendant light was making desperate efforts to resuscitate itself by periodical spasmodic jerks, I resolved, before we subsided into darkness, to have another look at Percy, and see, as far as I could judge, how matters really stood. Slowly and gently raising myself in bed, I bent over my friend, hoping to find him soundly sleeping; but his large eyes were gazing meditatively into mine, and, as it were, contemplating what was passing within me. For a moment we looked in silence at each other. I was endeavouring to read his thoughts, to anticipate his wants and wishes, thinking to lay down some well-devised plan for checking the consuming fever, that I felt was insidiously beginning its devouring work through all the ramifications of his veins, when he put forth his hand, took mine in his, and said,—

"I have seen her, old boy."

"Whom have you seen, Percy?"

" My—" he paused.

" My what ? " I continued.

" My—my—Nora," softly.

" Of course you have, old fellow, many, many times," I replied. " Turn on your side, lad, and endeavour to sleep, for you may require some strength to-morrow, ere the sun rise over the brow of the east hill."

" You mistake me, Oliver."

" I don't, upon my soul. Go to sleep," I said.

" I tell you Oliver, I saw her, yes, as plainly as I see you at this moment. It is no delusion of the brain ; I have not closed my eyes to-night, therefore it is no dream, wild imagination, or flight of the senses. I saw her—yes I saw her,—oh, that look ! that placid angelic look. She came dressed as a bride adorned for her husband, to show me the plain circle of gold around her finger. It was a little worn ;—a keeper, too—I placed them there. I gave her the watchword, yes, the same as we agreed upon, long, long ago, when we sat in the shrubbery, and the lark, as it were, heard the vows that were solemnly plighted, thrilling his delicious notes, shooting higher and higher into the dusky vault above, and warbling the glad tidings of our love to the angels in heaven. Oh! that watchword !—it was—"

He stopped, it was a full stop, marked with peculiar emphasis.

"What was it, Percy?" I said, having now no doubt in my mind that approaching symptoms of a bad fever were surely doing their mischievous and deadly work.

"Some other day, Oliver. I—I—I mean some other hour," significantly.

"I wish you fellows would 'shut up' your intolerable noise. Who on earth can sleep whilst you two are 'jawing' away at this hour?" said Lieutenant ——, who was sharing our tent, and whose presence during the whole of the night, was particularly conspicuous, in consequence of his sonorous renderings in sundry snoring duets with Captain ———.

I was too much occupied with more serious thoughts to make any reply at the moment, but quietly slipping out of bed, throwing a military cloak over my shoulders, and jumping into my long regulation boots, I glided out of the tent, determined to look up the doctor, who was sleeping in his own quarters, some distance off near the staff.

The moon, which had been skulking most of the night behind some ominous-looking dark clouds, was now slowly disappearing, and the grey streaks of the earliest dawn were forcing their way, almost imperceptibly, through the long mass of straggling, travelling, dismal-looking scuds, that were floating away in the dusky firmament with the northerly breeze.

With a light step, but heavy heart, I rapidly wended my way through the group of white tents that were spotted about in all directions.

I had not travelled far, and was certainly not absent long, when my attention was suddenly arrested by the firing of shots by the outposts; it was repeated again and again. In a few moments the bugle sounded—" To horse." Good heavens! I held my breath to listen. Yes, 'tis true, there is no mistaking those sounds; even the very animals snort and paw the ground in eager anticipation of what is to follow. 'Tis too true, the Russians in considerable force are sweeping down on us, not two miles distant; no time was to be lost. I made a dash for our tent, and on my arrival I found my orderly with first charger buckling up the second girth. Such was our system and discipline, that we were rarely if ever caught " napping."

I rushed into the tent, and shouted,— " Percy, Percy ; Lieutenant Snowdon, where is Lieutenant Snowdon ? "

" In his saddle, sir, bringing up his men and waiting orders," was the prompt reply of the sergeant-major, who had just galloped in.

Two more well-known sounds of the bugle, and saddles are filled ; cavalry sweep round, infantry come on at the double, column after column, with great impetuosity. The bugle again sounds in another direction, more men leap into their saddles ; endless jerks of horses as they spring into collars ; rattling of chains, limbering of guns, ammunition and ambulance waggons ; every man is at his post like clock-work, dashing away, and we are face to face with the enemy, who had stealthily crept on under cover of night, in the hope of finding our division unprepared for an attack, instead of which we were "all there," and not only so, but, in camp phraseology, "fresh as paint," and "fit."

I found that Lieutenant Snowdon had his men well in hand. He sat his charger, notwithstanding his illness, as "firm as a rock;" but I could see when he saluted me on my giving orders, that his cheeks looked as crimson as the red sun that was slowly rising, so to speak, out of the bowels of the earth, taking a last look at the glittering belt of steel and mass of human beings that hurried up with great speed. We were under orders to charge "Slaughter Hill" (as we afterwards dubbed it), an important position, which was already bristling with thousands of Russian bayonets; the bright steel of the swords and helmets flashed, and told their own peculiar tale of impending horror. Our riflemen, or sharp-shooters, were spread out in all directions; they had commenced their "picking off" work of destruction, and had already emptied many a saddle of its brave occupant.

Just before the —th field battery received orders to commence operations, and cover us in the work we had to do, I heard Lieutenant Snowdon distinctly say to the men, in a low but audible voice, as he gaily trotted up, threading in and out of the ranks, a few significant monosyllables. The words were,—

"Men, be *firm as a rock.*" Percy knew too well (no one better) that we were under orders to do a "big thing!"

"Lieutenant Snowdon," I said, galloping up to him, "you are—" I hesitated. I was on the point of commanding him to fall out and proceed to hospital, for manifestly the fever was on him. "Lieutenant Snowdon," I continued, gaining fresh courage, and taking advantage of a momentary lull, "you are ill; you had better—"

"Never better in my life, sir; never so fit," was the prompt reply, accompanied by the usual salute.

I wish to heaven I had been firm in my first resolution; but a cheer from the front rank (though contrary to strict discipline) and a murmur of approval from some officers close by, at the conclusion of Lieutenant Snowdon's words, prevented my saying more. The flash of his eyes, lit up the hateful hectic flush on his cheeks, told me plainly what was passing within,—the war notes had vibrated, and he would not be denied.

At this moment General ——'s aide-de-camp cantered up and gave pressing orders.

"Never!" I said. "Impossible!"

"Those are my instructions, sir."

"Are you positive?" I replied.

" Positive, sir."

" Will admit of no doubt ?"

" None whatever, sir."

" Repeat them, please, in the presence of Lieutenant Snowdon."

As the step to be taken was unusually dangerous, and sheer madness (as I thought) to attempt, I was sceptical. The order being repeated and ratified by another aide-de-camp, I passed it to my subaltern and brave fellows ; then, ramming spurs into my charger, and holding them well in the sore, we dashed headlong into the most desperate struggle I encountered during the whole of the campaign.

I could give in detail a long and thrilling account of that ever - memorable and glorious charge ; but I pause, lest in doing so I should be building up, as it were, something which may come under the appellation of egotism. Therefore, all I say

is, that never in the history of any charge
upon record is there one to be accounted
more brilliant than that of my brave men
on the memorable —th. Alas! how few
there are left to tell the tale, and journey
with me again over the events of that
thrilling day. How I rejoice whenever I
meet one of those gallant fellows of highly-
tempered steel, those hearts of oak, who
bore, so to speak, a charmed life amidst
the hail of red-hot iron and torrents of
lead, as they cut in their mighty flight
long straight lanes in our ranks. But our
watchword was " Forward!" And in our
journey we staggered,—rallied,—wrenched!
and finally cheered one continuous cheer,
which echoed from hill to hill, and vied
with the thundering artillery that roared
in the distance, as it were, approvingly,
as our standard (shot into shreds) floated
triumphantly in the northerly breeze on the

top of the earthwork, and the ray of the morning sun pierced the dense volume of dusky smoke, which curled and curled into circles and semicircles, passing into infinitismal particles, exposing a plain of death and destruction!

I received two or three wounds, but, happily, felt nothing seriously shattered, neither had my limbs thoroughly given away. Several of my men rushed forward, and carried me off on their shoulders. I recollect " Big Paddy " (as he was jocosely called) saying.—" Bedad, captain, we will make sure of ye this time, anyhow, or, by the powers, a bit of a missinger will be coming this way, requiring your service in the other kingdom that is to come."

On my road to hospital I met Sergeant Gregory, spread on a litter. He had distinguished himself immensely. I said, cheerfully,—

"Hulloa, sergeant! where are you going, lad?"

"Homeward bound, sir," was the prompt reply.

"Are you much hurt?" I continued.

"I have dropped an arm somewhere, sir, on the road; but it don't much matter, captain, I sha'n't want it again," he replied, with great *sang froid.*

"Brave fellow," I said, at the same time eagerly asking him if he had seen Lieutenant Snowdon.

"Down, sir, down. Dead as a door nail."

"How—when—where?" I asked.

Poor Sergeant Gregory had said all he had to say in this world, fired his last shot; his last cartridge was spent. He fainted—it was a long swoon, through a long valley, from which he never returned.

"Big Paddy" and others carried me to

camp. The doctor soon removed my uni-
form, sewed up a small aperture or two ;
all of which, except loss of blood, were, I
thought at the time, apparently trifling
matters, and he ordered me to hospital ;
but as I felt I had not finished my work
for the day, I would not hear of it, so wrig-
gling again into my deeply-stained garments,
taking a long and strong pull at the brandy
flask, also the arm of our kind-hearted and
estimable doctor, I proceeded in search of
poor Percy.

It was a dismal journey, limping along
amongst heaps of dead and dying, seeking
for one of the best fellows in creation ; but I
felt, notwithstanding poor Gregory's informa-
mation as to the " door nail," that there was
just a chance of finding him living ; and
such proved to be the case, for in a few
moments I espied his grey charger, doubled
up, and occasionally making desperate plunges

to get upon his legs, but, with his hind limb completely shattered, the poor brute found it a physical impossibility to accomplish. About fifty yards from the animal, I discovered Percy, seated on the ground, leaning his head on the breast of a gunner, who was bathing his temples, and doing his best to keep life in him.

The moment I set eyes on my friend, I knew that he had received "notice to quit," for I had too much experience in such matters. The death-like cast of countenance, the film over the eyes, peculiar hue on the lips, cold perspiration, and other signs, were all unmistakable evidences of a speedy dissolution.

The doctor placed his finger on his pulse, and whispered something dismally in my ear, —my worst fears were confirmed.

"Why, Percy, my dear old boy," I said, trying, with a jerk, to be cheerful, "what, taking your rest, lad, after a hard gallop?"

The sound of my voice rallied him wonderfully.

"What has given way?" I asked, smoothing my hand across his handsome, marble-like forehead, and wiping the perspiration from his face with my handkerchief.

He looked up, smiled, and said,—

"Only scratched."

"Where?" I eagerly asked, endeavouring to ascertain for myself the extent of his injury, ignoring altogether, in my anxiety, the presence of the surgeon.

"Only tapped one of my lungs, that's all," he replied.

By this time the surgeon knew all about it, and had prepared a capital arrangement, on which my poor dying subaltern was placed, and carried away by four stalwart fellows to my tent, where the doctor undressed him, and found a small wound in the right breast. On further examination, a corresponding wound was seen near the blade bone, evidently caused by a bullet passing, in its onward course, completely through the lung; but, strange to say, there was scarcely any external hæmorrhage.

After propping him well up, and the surgeon having given him a powerful restorative, I took the latter on one side, and asked him what he thought of the case.

"He may live an hour or so," was the reply.

"Not longer?" I ventured.

"Can't say; the whole thing is very problematical; he is bleeding internally, and nothing can be done for him," replied the surgeon, hurrying off to attend scores of other cases that demanded immediate attention.

I took my camp chair and placed it by the side of poor Percy's bed.

"Are you thirsty, my dear old boy!" I asked.

"Very," was the meek and feeble rejoinder; "but I know something that will help to quench it."

I was about to prepare a refreshing draught, when he took from under his pillow a small pocket Bible, and handed it to me. I knew what he wanted. I opened the book where a marker was placed, the latter being a strip of perforated cardboard, used by ladies in their fancy needlework, on which were a cross and the words, "Firm as a Rock;" also in the margin of the sacred book there was sketched a small hand, which pointed to the fifty-fifth chapter of Isaiah,—"Ho every one that thirsteth," etc.

I read him, at his request, the chapter partly through, when he stopped me, and said, in a scarcely audible voice,—

"Oliver, I am loath to interrupt you, for

I could listen, were I permitted, to those comforting words for hours, but hours are not for me—barely minutes."

He paused for a while ; I bathed his temples, lifted him higher upon the pillow ; I was nearly choking, but did not dare to speak, being anxious to drink in every word he had breath left to give utterance to.

His faithful servant, Martin, was standing at the foot of the bed. Percy motioned him to leave the tent, when he slowly continued,—

" My dear old boy, the Author of that book, from which you have just read, is now about to fulfil His promise. He is going to present me with a new life in exchange for the old one."

Another long pause ; I could not reply. Unhappily, I felt out of my depth ; his researches in that Holy Book, my shortcomings; his eyes open, mine closed; his perception clear, mine cloudy, are wholesome facts, established, I trust, in my memory for ever.

He continued very slowly,—

"I have endeavoured, Oliver, to keep good company in this world, but I hope soon to move in better, and more lasting. I am enduring at this moment three distinct wrenches. I—I—"

I administered some brandy, and with it a bumping tear, that somehow or other promiscuously rolled into the glass, which I am not ashamed to own, for if ever in this world a tear of friendship tumbled out of the eye of man, I shed one then.

Poor Percy had no tears left, they were all " wiped away from his eyes." The stimulant I administered somewhat revived him, and he continued,—

" I have three wrenches—three loved ones

to part with, Oliver "— and, taking the locket from his breast, where it hung by a piece of black ribbon, he touched the spring; it flew open, and putting it to his lips again and again, clasped his hands together, apparently in great agony of mind, uttering feebly the following words :—" My Nora—my—my—yes. My—and yet not my—"

" Your what ? " I whispered entreatingly.

" My—never mind ; come nearer, old boy, nearer still ; put your head close to mine."

Thinking that he wished to communicate something of importance, I placed my ear near his mouth, when he threw the ribbon around my neck, attached to which was the locket holding Nora's portrait, saying,—

" Wear it, Oliver—this ' Shadow in the Gold '—wear it for my sake, and when you

look on the reflex of the fair face of my
Nora in that little circle, it may remind
you of the closest and dearest tie of your
devoted friend. Should you in your travels,
find yourself face to face with the original,
give her this Bible and marker, and say
that the former was the most precious gift
I ever possessed ; tell her it proved a healing balm to the ugly wound here ; and it
has fortified my soul for its journey through
the long valley I am now entering."

"Anything more can I say ?" I interrupted dismally.

"Yes, yes, something more, though but
little ; yet much—post this letter ; and should
you meet my Nora, say—say—'Firm as a
Rock.'"

"Anything more, dear Percy ?"

"Not in that quarter. I have disposed
of one matter, and there is not much time
left for me. Give my fondest love to the

darling who gave me birth ; tell her that
I have endeavoured to keep the name I
own without blemish, and those early and
loving admonitions which she inculcated into
my mind, have proved of inestimable value
in my journey to the threshold of my
new and eternal home, to which I am
now hastening."

Perceiving that he was fast sinking, I
entreated him to be quiet and rest a
while, when he held up his finger, and
continued,—

"It is nearly finished. I have but one
more wrench, and that is parting from you
my friend, my faithful, devoted companion."

"God bless you, Percy," I stammered.

"He has blessed me," replied Percy,
with a voice scarcely audible. "I am as
happy, Oliver, as the sweetest songster that
ever soar'd in yon firmament, and I owe
it all to that blessed Book—my mother's

tender and careful development, and my—
my—yes, my Nora.   Don't forget to—to
tell her—' Firm as a—a—a—Rock.' ''

I am alone with the corpse of the once
brave and faithful Percival Snowdon.

CHAPTER III.

MY LAST DAY ON THE BATTLEFIELD.

ERECT I stood, folded my arms, and gazed a long abstracted gaze on the lifeless form of my departed friend, who, a few moments before, breathed forth such sensible and loving words; who so recently mingled, heart and soul, in the battle fray, and carried (with a handful of men) all before him, now for ever beyond the reach of further shot and shell.

Alone with the dead!

One would imagine that death at this juncture could be nothing to me, could create no unusual sensation of horror other than that which always associates itself with the battlefield. I had only to wander a few steps from my tent and witness it in all its appalling and ghastly form, piled up in places waist deep ; surely, then, it would seem to a superficial observer that death could be nothing to me in the midst of broad acres of it lying scattered here and there ; what, then, was the meaning of those bumping tears ? I imagine I hear some fellow say (who may one day ramble promiscuously over these pages), " A soldier's tear indeed ! and on the battlefield, too ! All bosh ! moonshine ! sensational ! "

I fancy, too, that there may be—nay, I will take it for granted, there will be others who will dip into this narrative with something more than a cursory glance, and shed tears to the memory of the brave ; those beloved ones whom they have lost on the plains of a battlefield ;—

a husband, father, brother, son, or true friend.

Such readers will have the clearest possible conception of the intensity of my feelings, as I stood bending over the inanimate form of my once brave companion and faithful colleague, realising my loss, and contemplating the havoc which a few short hours had made, robbing parents of a loving and promising son; a fond girl of her lover; his country of a host in himself; and your humble servant of a friend!

"Poor Percy!" I muttered in half-broken accents, the mighty roar and swing of the battlefield, seeking for glory and honour! "Now thou art gone, it will be sorry work for me. I have lost a stimulant that always spurred me on the road to victory; an example that helped me to earn some little distinction on the battlefield." How anxiously he looked forward to promotion ; how his eyes used to sparkle with delight when he contemplated it, and spoke of his Nora sharing with him the honours ; how rejoiced he was when I stepped up the ladder,—noble, unselfish fellow ! He has his reward, though else-where, on the " staff " above those azure skies ; he is promoted to a rank consider-ably higher than our gracious sovereign could have bestowed upon him. Had he lived, a Victoria cross would, assuredly, have adorned his breast. There is, how-ever, another cross, infinitely greater, of inestimable value, and far more precious, that is now, doubtless, his ; a glory, too, that awaited him, surpassing all knowledge ; a glory which illuminates a crown set with gems of his own procuring on earth. Jewels of the first water that from time to time he picked up, here and there, amongst some of the ungodly rabble of our army, whom he converted from the paths of dissipation ; gems of unknown worth, lustrous beyond description, all cut into the most beautiful facets, and set by the hand of the greatest lapidary.

> Who cares to seek the world's renown,
>   Such products of mortality ;
> With such a cross, and such a crown,
>   There's nothing like reality.

I felt lost in profound reverie when a hand was placed on my shoulder : it was the doctor, together with the sergeant-major, quarter-master sergeant, and four drummers ; verily, a procession of dismal undertakers, with their impromptu bier !

Typhus fever rendered it absolutely necessary that there should be a speedy burial; indeed, the stringent rules laid down admitted of no elasticity in our arrangements, neither was it desirable, under the circumstances, that there should be any delay.

It was a dismal, slow march as we conveyed the remains of Lieutenant Snowdon to his last six feet of narrow soil for the repose of his bones, over the very ground he galloped with his men but a few hours before with so much dash : a large number of dead were still scattered about in all directions, heaped up where they fell, in all manner of forms, standing out in bold relief on the brow of the hill, fitting monuments of the ghastly carnage that had made many a beloved wife a widow, and many a child fatherless. We laid him with pride and sadness in a narrow grave, with his arms folded on his breast. I took one long look at that placid face, lit up, though in death, with a beautiful smile which seemed to strike the chords of my heart, and speak one last farewell, when a military cloak was thrown over the body, and shut out, for ever, in this world, the once bright

and happy face of Lieutenant Percival
Snowdon.

A firing party of our best and oldest
men completed the only outward honours
that could be offered to the brave hero of
"Slaughter Hill;" but, within those massive
veteran heads, that bent silently over the
grave, there could be found some good
material; loving thoughts, too, were working in their own form and fashion; and
within those sadly worn and sunken eyes,
there were, undoubtedly, manifestations of
grief and solemnity.

> Beside that little grave,
> Stood many a warrior brave,
> With frames as hard as steel,
> But hearts that fondly feel.

Yes, many bumping tears glistened in
the sunshine that morning, and were brushed
away by the hard brown hands of those men,
as they looked down for the last time on

the form that led them so nobly to victory, earning for himself such distinction, and whose memory will be handed down to posterity.

> And they turn'd their heads away
>   From the form they held so dear,
> "And lent upon their rifles,
>   And wiped away a tear."

.   .   .   .

Enough—death-bed scenes, ghastly sights, and alarming events are not altogether inviting themes to dwell upon in any narrative, but, in compiling the reminiscences of these memorable days, I do so as the only tribute I can offer to the brave hero of "Slaughter Hill," and I shall cherish up in my heart, with a loving remembrance, the joys and pleasures of our young, and be it said, active, happy life, on duty and off duty, at home and abroad; in doing so, I look back with the most lively satisfaction, and can safely place it on record, that Percival Snowdon's friendship was faithful—yes—"Firm as a Rock."

Should the reader, in his travels, ever reach that corner of the Crimea, the plot of sacred ground which no Englishman can regard without feelings of pride and sadness, the last resting-place of many departed heroes of the campaign, he may, perchance, drop a silent tear over the spot where

"The flowers of the country entwine o'er his grave."

·   ·   ·   ·   ·   ·   ·   ·   ·

I directed my steps towards our tent, for, by this time, I found my wounds "crying aloud for help;" feeling faint, weak, and low in spirits, I threw myself on my camp bed-stead, and requested the attendance of the surgeon, who promptly came to my assistance. As night drew on, feverish symptoms of a violent character presented themselves,

followed by delirium, which stubbornly continued for a long period—battles were fought,
lost and won, marching and counter-march-
ing proceeded ; it made, however, little difference to me, for I was utterly incapable
of knowing anything that was going on
from the 8th to the 19th. On the morning of the latter day, I awoke, as it were,
from a dream, the outcome of a second
attack of the same description of fever I
had before experienced, and which was
considerably aggravated by the painful
scenes I had recently passed through—my
wounds, loss of blood, exposure to bitterly
cold weather, and various privations consequent on the rapid and uncertain movements
of our army.

When I opened my eyes, with fairly
healthy faculties, I saw my faithful Irish
servant Curtis busily engaged in preparing
a compress, and soaking it in a chloroform

compound, or some such mixture, and at intervals slowly apostrophising a few words in a mechanical sort of way.

I could discern through my casement the hard lines of the mountainous hills, and their undulations standing out prominently, with their summits tipped with pyramids of driven snow, which sparkled in the rays of the morning sun, and seemed to vie with the white silvery scuds as they floated promiscuously in the firmament, casting their shadows in long streaks in the valley beneath. Some cattle were browsing on the slopes, vigorously nipping off, with determined jerks, the scant, russet-brown herbage on which they were pasturing; the juvenile and more agile herd were gamboling with each other merrily up and down the side-land, butting, leaping, playfully biting, and enjoying other frolics. My eyes wandered from one object to another, whilst Curtis, who had hold of his lip between his teeth, seemed lost in thought.

"Where on earth can I be?" I muttered; "not on the battle - field for certain, for I am in a quaint-looking room in some farm-house, a Russian one too, judging from the peculiar furniture that is arranged about the place. I am not altogether with strangers, for there is Curtis, my old and valued Irish servant. There are no sudden clouds and whiffs of that everlasting gunpowder, which, for months past, I had been inhaling. No bugle sounds, roaring of mortars, howitzers, tramping of regiments, roll of fife and drum, galloping of horses, rattling of chains, piling arms, and other sounds so familiar to my ear; all, except the frolicsome cattle in the sideland close by, and the monotonous bleating of sheep, was as still as the grave. Even my servant seemed to have suddenly subsided into a piece of domestic furniture;

but for a deep sigh which I heard the poor fellow " dig up," I should almost have thought he had been transmogrified into the traditional pillar !

" Lost anything ? " I said, in a feeble voice.

" Oh, good Lord ! by the powers ! who's that ? " was the reply.

" Where the deuce am I, Curtis ? "

" Lord bless ye, master ! by the powers ! if I didn't jist about think ye were well nigh in distant lands ; sure alive, I'm glad ye are come to life again.   All I have to say is, lie still, or ye will be jist going off again on your old rounds for sure, and there will be no stopping ye."

" Where am I, Curtis ? " I continue.

" Faith, in good quarters, anyhow ; and be satisfied, captain, and don't be after asking any more questions."

" If you will only—"

Weakness asserted its rights, and arrested my speech.

"To be sure I will," replied Curtis, sharply, taking up the "running"; "jist anything in this blessed world, if ye will only jist turn round on that pleasant little heart of your own, and be still as a mouse in a corner for an hour, and I will be fitching someone to see ye, anyhow."

I squeezed the faithful fellow's hand, and felt thankful I was under his care; but a sudden termination of blood to the head affected my brain, a sharp spasm attacked my heart, followed by cold shivers. I closed my eyes, and sank again into an unconscious state.

History reports me to have swooned or slept the whole of that day and a part of the night. When I again opened my eyes, I found myself almost in total darkness. There was, however, a small glimmer of light which hailed from a smouldering log of wood in an arrangement which was suggestive of a fire-grate. I gazed a long time at the crimson spark that occasionally shot up and crackled in the stillness of the night, and collected my thoughts as well as I could. I felt much revived; the sound sleep had very considerably refreshed me. I could easily connect some past events and fairly well retain them without the risk of wandering. My wounds began to give me pain for the first time; this I considered a good sign. Having, in the most satisfactory manner, assured myself of this, I tried to penetrate the surrounding darkness and see how matters stood. Following the faint streak of red light from the embers that threw their dismal glimmer across the twelve-feet apartment in spasmodic jerks, it fell on a human face.

Such a face!

For the moment I was absorbed in endeavouring to trace the features. " Is it Curtis? No, it cannot be. Curtis hasn't long, black, flowing hair." I heard my heart thumping away with a peculiar thud. At this moment a burning ember slipped down. A red light suddenly revealed the features of a beautiful girl seated on the floor, her arms folded across her breast, and her large coal-black eyes wandered at intervals from me to the smouldering firewood. All was silent, except the monotonous tick, tick, tick of an old clock on the mantelpiece. Who hasn't at some period of his life felt an irresistible impression of some unknown influence steal over the soul, awaken and stir up the best feelings of our nature in a foreign land? Languishing on a bed of sickness, and amongst strangers, one would naturally feel all the force of love and gratitude for those who come to one's rescue, and, like ministering angels, keep watch through the night!

"My conscience!" I murmured, "who ever can it be?" As a kind of preliminary or notification of my existence in the world, I kicked the bedclothes, and cleared my throat with some emphasis. It had the desired effect, for the brunette was at my side in a moment.

I felt a soft hand pass gently over my forehead and press back the straggling hair that had promiscuously fallen over my brow.

"Where am I?" I softly asked, at the same time feebly taking hold of the wrist of the girl; "to whom am I indebted for such kindness?"

The nurse placed her finger vertically across her lips as a sign of silence, bathed my temples with some refreshing mixture, which sent forth a balmy odour, and then immediately left the apartment.

"Jewel!" I muttered.

In a few moments Curtis was at my side, groping away at my pulse, and blowing in my face like distraction.

"Try your bellows on the fire," I said, "and let us have some light on the subject."

"The Lord be praised!" ejaculated Curtis, clasping his hands, and making a desperate effort to relight the oil-lamp.

"Now, old fellow, where am I?" I asked.

"Faith now, ye'll have the politeness just to keep that little wandering musical tongue of yours quiet a bit, or, bedad, if ye won't be after yer old pranks, and leaving us in the lurch again, and going away on yer own 'hook' on another visit to that blessed Nora."

"Where? to whom?" I eagerly inquired, wiping a cold stream of perspiration from my forehead.

"I only wish the hussy and all her little bairns had been at the bottom of the briny sea, a-dancing 'Irish jigs like evermore' with the mermaids, than a-bothering yer honour with her tomfoolery from sunrise till sundown. Sure alive, ye haven't had a morsel of pace for her."

"What on earth are you talking about, Curtis ? "

"Never mind, master, for, sure then. Some fine evening I will be after a-telling ye all about it."

"You have greatly excited my curiosity, Curtis ; for heaven's sake tell me—"

"Excited yer what, did ye say? Bother! Just take a long pull at this 'pick me up' that the doctor left for ye a moon since, for ye to pay yer addresses to just when circumstances require it,—to be shaken before taken."

It is needless to add that I eagerly

drank the mixture.   Its magic influence
soon reported itself favourably to my poor
shattered nerves.   I rested awhile in deep
thought, meditating on the past, ponder-
ing over the brunette, and anticipating
the future.   At last I thought I would
try a little *finesse* with my servant, and
continued,—

"What about Flora, Curtis?"

"Bother," he replied, "ye know very
well ye haven't had any dealings with a
Flora at all; and my advice to ye, master,
is, that, judging from what I have been able
to 'pick out' on yer long journey, ye had
better cut that lady's company, for she hasn't
done ye any good, for cartain."

"But, Curtis," I feebly remonstrated, "I
don't know any such person as Nora; I
never saw her in my life," at the same
time asking for another dose of the cordial.

"Bother! sure, then, ye can recollect,

master, that 'tisn't Flora, anyhow; ye had just better be leaving off yer itemings, and compose yer dear self a bit, or I won't answer for the company ye'll be next keeping, if ye are off again on yer 'marching order;' sure alive, 'tis all 'open order' wid ye."

"I tell you, Curtis, I never saw Nora, that I know of."

"Nor her likeness, I suppose, that is tucked up so snug to yer heart under yer flannen waistcoat; and, by the powers! if the name N o r a isn't chiseled out at the back of it, and night after night ye have been crying out for the 'Shadow in the Gold.'"

After this piece , of elegant peroration, Curtis left the room, and I soon heard him conversing with some one downstairs, who was busily engaged in beating up an egg.

"Yes, sure enough, this is the identical picture," I soliloquised (as I drew forth Nora's portrait from its hiding-place), "that dear Percy, in the last moments of his life, threw around my neck, entreatingly asking me to wear it for his sake, and that if ever, in my travels, I came face to face with the original, to look upon her as his 'nearest and dearest tie'—how significant, 'nearest tie!'—two words suggestive of much."

I revolved in my mind all my early conversation with Percy, and connected one event with another; fitted link to link— one, however, was missing, an important one, too, in the chain of his life, which, alas! so soon parted.

Whilst I gazed on the reflex of the fair face of the "angel girl" (as Percy called her) in the circle of gold, I dwelt upon the memory of my lamented friend—of my affection for him—of his sincerity for me; and I was carried away to foreign climes, where we wandered together, and where he told, re-told, and never grew weary of relating, long joyous days he had passed in the society of his dearest Nora; the love that he had plighted, and how it had been accepted; the anguish they both experienced on separating; the secret—the grand secret of his life—that he said he had some day to impart to me. His last dying words are, and ever will be, uppermost in my thoughts. "Forget them? bid the forest birds forget their sweetest tune."

Those words! so full of touching sorrow, will ever live in my memory as

"As firm as a Rock."

CHAPTER IV.

———

WHO IS SHE?

A most uneventful week elapsed since the close of the last chapter, certainly so far as I was concerned ; but, in order that one may fairly well clear up straggling events as we proceed, and that there may be no unreasonable gap in my narrative, it is as well to explain to the reader exactly what happened after I succumbed to the violent fever on the memorable —th, when prostration and delirium set in. During the whole of that time, I am not aware of having experienced one rational moment, neither have I the remotest recollection of anything that occurred after my return from Percy's funeral.

I am informed by my servant Curtis that I first fainted, or, to use his own familiar words, "went clean off my head, sure;" he also reports that my mind travelled "heaven knows where." From the very lucid and graphic description he gave of the whole matter, I did not for a moment doubt his veracity.

The brilliant success of our battalion on the —th somewhat cleared the atmosphere, and a temporary lull ensued, the spell of which, however, was soon broken, for orders were given for a forced march on ——, to the immediate relief of General ——, who at that time was sorely pressed and losing ground. The desperate condition I was in, rendered it impossible to take me any great distance from the ground we then occupied, without imperiling my life. Jolting along rough roads, over a mountainous country, in an ambulance waggon, would, the doctor considered, have jolted out the last spark of life that was flickering within me ; and as I had contributed my fair share, conjointly with many brave fellows, towards the achievements of the last struggle with the enemy. Great anxiety, consideration, and forbearance were manifested by the " staff" on my behalf, consequently I was transferred from under canvas to a small Russian farm, situated about three miles distant from the scene of action. The colonel having previously solicited and obtained from the owner a faithful promise to thoroughly look after me, at the same time assuring him that " money was no object," a piece of information (coupled with a presentation of something tangible) that greatly accelerated the farmer's hospitable movements, wound up his generosity, and probably it was (in a great measure) the means of saving my life.

My old and valued servant Curtis, who had providentially managed through the campaign to keep clear of the leaden messengers of death, and who also escaped the distressing cholera and fever then prevailing, was told off to wait upon me. Sundry well-known specifics in the way of physic, with almost every conceivable restorative that the kind-hearted and estimable Doctor —— could think of, and spare from his store, together with minute written instructions, were left with Curtis, who, in the most indefatigable manner, discharged the duties entrusted to him ; and a good Samaritan he proved to be, for through long days and lonely nights his sleepless eyes watched over my burning frame.

Also the dear girl of whom I shall have the privilege of speaking, joined hand to hand in the labour that my desperate state of health forced upon them, and through dint of the greatest care and watchfulness, contrived, with God's blessing, to pull me through; and I rejoice in making a record in these pages, of my everlasting indebtedness to my faithful old servant Curtis, and the beautiful little brunette of ——, for their loving and untiring attention to the wants of a helpless, wounded, fever-stricken soldier; whilst life exists, Heaven knows, that my gratitude will be lasting!

In the course of time, I gained sufficient strength to bear the fatigue of being dressed by my Irish valet, who, by-the-bye, was uncommonly shy of conversing upon any subject whatever; from what I gathered, he had received positive orders not to talk in my presence, or permit me to do so, and as my excessive weakness rendered every word I uttered distressing, it is not at all surprising that I greatly preferred quietude.

For hours together I sat in my little room wrapped in meditation, sometimes sinking down in the troubled waters of this life; at others, building "castles in the air," in lively anticipation of the future, and earnestly longing to be on the move, at the head of my brave fellows again; but the fetters of disease and my wounds arrested my best resolutions and damped my ardour, but a renewal of hope gave consolation.

I had a few books with me, notably a small pocket edition of Shakespeare, my *vade-mecum*, which was a library in itself —a "crumb of comfort" in health and in sickness; there was another book too in my possession, of which I have previously spoken; it had a marker in it. I held it in trust, to be delivered to Nora. I don't quite know why, but certainly there was a charm about that little volume, an irresistible attraction, a magnetic influence that bound me, as it were, to every leaf; sensitively operating upon, and working a mighty power within me, such as I never before experienced. Was it the outcome of the struggle that I recently passed through between life and death? Was it the outcome of the reminiscences of my lamented friend?— or was it the outcome of the anticipation of some day taking the hand of the fair owner of that sacred book and marker, and depositing its wealth within her tiny grasp, and personally delivering her lover's last words,— " Firm as a Rock " ? I pause—and will leave it where it is for the present, to be revealed, as far as it can be made manifest, in the pages that are to follow.

.   .   .   .

A gentle knock at the door.

" Come in ; is that you, Curtis ? "

"And sure 'tis my viry own self, yer honour," was the reply.

"Come here, Curtis; sit down, I want to talk with you."

"Then, indeed to goodness, ye are jist viry much mistaken, if ye think I am arrived here to hold gossip with ye, anyhow, for ye are not strong enough, captain, in the back yet; and the doctor jist about gave me orders not to have yer tongue middled with; and bother, if that Nora isn't after ye, directly ye close yer weary eyes in the cradle of sleep, and yer cheeks get like thumping red potatoes. Sure she is no good company, anyhow; bad luck to her, and—" .

"I request that you discontinue such remarks, Curtis," I vehemently replied, "and speak not lightly of that name."

"Och! bother! then I know master, now, which way the wind blows; the little straw that I threw up caught well in the breeze, and faith I know which way it is flying."

"Hush!" I say; "you annoy me. I'll have no more of it. Who was that gipsy-looking woman that I saw sitting in my bedroom, maybe days, weeks, perhaps months since? for, alas! of late I have kept no reckoning of time."

A long pause—no reply.

"Do you hear me, Curtis?"

"Never heard anything plainer, sir."

"Tell me then," sharply.

"Woman did ye say, yer honour?"

"Yes; that very dark woman, who sat up with me, bathed my temples, quenched my thirst with a cooling draught, knelt at my bedside; and, although I addressed her, she positively left the room without uttering a word."

"Sure, then, it wasn't a woman at all."

"You perverter of the truth!" I exclaimed, in the most irritable manner; "do you think that disease has so robbed me of my senses that I do not know a man from a woman?"

"Sure, then, it wasn't a woman at all, I tell ye agin."

"Then you tell me a lie—a wicked—"

"Faith, yer honour, by the powers! I wouldn't take sich an unwarrantable liberty with ye, or with any creature under the sun."

"Who then was it, you idiot, that sat at my bedside? Was it a man, woman, beast, angel, or the ——" I replied, savagely.

"Neither the one nor the other, master."

"Then I was dreaming," I said.

"Niver wider awake in yer life, master, than ye were that blissed night."

"Then I was mad; yes, mad as a march hare."

"Niver more sane in yer life, captain," was the laconic reply.

I suggested, by way of a last gasp, that

it was a ghost paying her nocturnal visits, and, in my then hasty and irritable temper, was about to show the fellow the door, when he continued,—

" Sure then, yer honour, I have tazed ye enough ; but I vintured to hope, with the very best intentions, so that I should jist about steer ye clear of the information ye are after. But, as ye won't take *no* for an answer, I'll be after telling ye, by way of a short cut, jist a morsel of the knowledge ye are fishing with yer hook for ; but ye haven't got the proper bait at the end of yer line, and the fish won't bite ; and if it would, ye haven't got the strength to take it, and land it ; but as ye have jist about tickled the trout, I'll help ye with my landing-net, and give ye a peep at her fin."

" All right," I replied ; " proceed."

" The woman ye spake of isn't a woman at all."

" What then ?   Come now, Curtis," entreatingly.

" Sure, then, it was a lady," he continued, at the same time grinning, and
displaying a set of the most irregular
teeth.

" A lady ! " I exclaimed.

" Faith, a live lady ! "

" But a lady is a woman," I replied ;
" did I not declare that—"

" But a woman, your honour—excuse my
liberty—isn't always a lady in our country ;
and we wouldn't offer such a hastily com-
pliment to highborn persons in County Kil-
dare as to call a lady a woman."

" Lady ! who ? — what ! where is she ? "
I asked, in one breath. " Keep me no
longer in suspense."

" There's your thumping red potatoes
coming again, like flashes of fork-lightning,
in your face, and the perspiring properties

are standing like marrapat peas on your forehead. If ye bother me so, yer honour, I'll be just after leaving ye to yer own reflections.

"Where is that lady, and who is she?" I again asked, at the same time helping myself to a drop more brandy, by way of fortifying myself for the climax; but, as per usual, the old man gently put a stopper on the supply.

"Fellow!" I continued, "where is she?"

"Oddfellow you mean, yer honour; sure, then, I belong to the ancient order of Foresters, and I carry the staff and banner of old Ireland and liberty for ever."

"Good Curtis," I responded, and awaited the continuation of his narrative.

"Now you promise, captain, to be very quiet, and dhrop all your excitement?"

"I promise," I replied, familiarly slapping

the fellow's shoulder as an earnest of my good-feeling.

"Hearken, then. That live lady that ye saw when ye 'come to' in the middle of that bitter night, when the flakes of snow were falling fast and thick, and the howling wind was blowing straight from the steppes of Scythia, is lying—"

"Lying where?" I shouted.

"Lying downstairs, captain."

"What!" I gasped; "not dead?"

"Not yet; but I don't quite know, captain, how long it will be before her darling soul takes flight, for she has been almost devoured by inches with the horrid fever she took of ye, and no mistake."

"Good heavens! let me go to her, without a moment's delay, and see for myself," I exclaimed, springing vigorously to my feet.

"I have locked the door, yer honour; and what is more, I have got the key in

my pocket, so ye jist can't go anyhow,"
said Curtis.

"I am well, man, I am well; I am as
strong as a lion, and as—'

"Weak as a little 'ba-lamb,'" was Curtis's
rejoinder. "No, yer honor, ye must be
quiet, and all may come right and tight in a
little while. The 'broth' of a child is just
a shade better this morning; and when she
tossed up her black eyes, I fancied she knew
me a little bit, the darling, she did, sure."

"Her name?" I asked wildly, clutching
the wrist of my servant with some earnestness.

"Constance Templar; and a mighty good
templar she has proved herself to be, anyhow."

"Ministering angels protect her!" I exclaimed.

"The Red Cross, yer honour."

"The Red Cross! Constance Templar!
Cannot be true, man, cannot be. How is it

she sojourns here, and why is she not with the army ? "

" Miss Templar was invalided, master, and found refuge in this farmhouse before ye were brought here. She was getting better, and preparing for another flight and fresh work with the division; but when we carried ye up the steps on a litter, she met yer honour's body at the porch, and she sighed a long, deep, heavy sort of sigh, like my poor Biddy of Tipperary used to do, and said she had her work cut out again, and she made a vow that she would not leave what was left of the noble hero of 'Slaughter Hill,' as she called ye, until she had landed ye high and dry, or put ye in 'port' in yer last little home,—the darling! that's what she did, sure! And anyhow, she kept her word, for she took her turn day and night, and did for ye, faith, like a tinder mother would do for her sickly babe. From sunrise to sundown

she was on the watch. When the moon
rose, she rose ; and the night and the day
was niver too long for her ; but the darling
daisy was soon cut down, and she began to
wither like the pritty flowers that she placed
on yer honour's bed. Scorched and burnt
almost to death by the raging fever, she tossed
her little restless bones about on her hard
couch ; and the Russian mother downstairs,
bless her ! has taken her under her wings day
and night, and kept her body and soul together."

There was a long pause following this
painful and sensational narrative ; a dismal
lookout over the broad plain. Curtis's head
was turned one way, mine another. Neither
of us wished to portray what was passing
within our hearts, — gathering within the
folds of our eyelids, or show, in any way,
the reflex of our thoughts.

But poor Curtis buried his face in his
big brown hand, and wept like a child.

CHAPTER V.

MY OWN REFLECTIONS, AND WHAT FOLLOWED.

"To be found untired,
Watching the stars out by the bed of pain,
With a pale cheek, and yet a brow inspired,
And a true heart of hope; though hope be vain.
Meekly to bear with wrong, to cheer decay,
And oh! to live through all things,—therefore pray!"

Mrs Hemans.

I AM alone,—left, as Curtis remarked, "to my own reflections." The Irish valet has taken my wounded surviving charger for "an airing.' As the poor brute limped along under my lattice window, with several ugly wounds staring me in the face, I almost wished, at the moment, I had given him his *coup-de-grâce* on the —th, and thus ended his military career and misery for ever; but,

on second consideration, I was anxious to
take the noble steed to the home of my
fathers; for bravely he carried me through
torrents of shot and fire,—"landing" me
safely at last.

"No," I said to myself, " we will not part.
If I can heal thy wounds, which, like my own,
seem stubborn enough, I will journey with
thee once more to the front, and again try
our luck; but if fate should decide against
us, and we don't put our harness together in
volumes of smoke, then, I say, in ' volumes '
of type thy deeds, ' Rob Roy,' shall be recorded.   Poor brute ! thou cannot speak for
thyself, but happily thy master, who knows
thy worth, is spared to sound the trumpet
boldly, and sing thy praises for thee,—gay,
springy, plucky, light-mouthed ' Rob Roy ; '
the very paragon of a horse in all thy paces ;
thy good manners and fearless dash are well
known ; when thou art grown old, thy bright

eyes dim, and thou art unable to carry me, then on the green pastures of our home park, under the shadow of thy master's house thou shalt graze, and spend the residue of thy life undisturbed."

Alone with my own reflections !

What are they ? Torrents of thought pour upon me !

I have suddenly experienced a heavy weight —a responsibility which is quite new. I have a duty to perform—a duty which has devolved upon me by sheer accident ; I have a debt to pay—a debt of gratitude. God willing, I will discharge the obligation I owe to the uttermost.

Yes, downstairs, according to my servant's description, there is the dear girl who, through long days and nights, tenderly watched over and nursed me, and exposed herself to the treacherous disease that was hourly consuming my body,—which malady she has taken

in its most violent form,—whilst the object of
her care has been spared to tell this narrative.

I revolve it all in my mind, and seriously
ponder over the best means to adopt in the
hope of restoring Miss Templar to health.
Though excessively weak, I am much better.
I must see her at once, and judge for myself. A medical man must be procured without loss of time. She may have a fond
mother, whose prayers invoke Heaven for her
child far away; she may have a father proud
of his daughter's glory and honour, with a
heart overflowing with affection for her safety
on the battle-field; a lover too, who— I
pause in my meditation, and take another
long look out over the snow-clad land in the
distance, rising, as it were, by gentle and im-
perceptible degrees, and which every day dis-
plays some new feature of beauty and sub-
limity, with interminable ranges of coast, and
promontory after promontory.

Curtis is away with " Rob Roy." I'll grope my way downstairs, and find the Russian mother, who shall at once take me to the bedside of the fever-stricken girl.

Suiting the action to the apostrophised words, I seized my impromptu crutches, took a nip of cogniac, and was soon at the bottom of the winding staircase, where I stopped awhile to take breath. The door in the passage was open ; and I shall not readily forget how rejoiced I was when I felt the light, renovating air from the hills pouring down on my pale face. How delicious ! How invigorating ! I suddenly seemed to leap from a sick couch, at a bound, into the open, and lo ! I breathed again.

A girl was on her knees in the porch, whitening the flagstones ; an exorbitant black cat approached, familiarly raised her back and tail in the most insinuating manner,—voluntarily introducing herself to my notice by vigorously brushing my leg with her sleek side, which piece of performance she coaxingly repeated several times. I, of course, recognise her endearment, not by a kick, but a good fondle in my arms. We twain were particular friends from that hour! The girl at last observed me. She sprang to her feet, and, in her haste to beat a rapid retreat, upset the galvanised pail of water. I motioned her to stop, but she flew the faster; and I heard her gibbering away in the Russian tongue to someone in the dairy.

Soon a short, comely woman, with an exceedingly short dress, came forth, and, dropping a curtsey, made signs (by lifting her hands and arching her eyebrows) of evident amazement at my venturing out alone in such a weak state. In fact it was manifest that she considered me a most refractory invalid, and wound up the whole performance by good-temperedly shaking her head in a most suggestive way. She then led me into her spacious kitchen, in the corner of which, ensconced in an enormous fireplace, sat the provident farmer, smoking his pipe; and on either knee frolicked a curly-headed, bouncing boy, both rubicund, and looking the picture of health. On observing me, the father made a peculiar grunt of recognition. Judging from the sound, one would imagine that he had acquired it by being constantly in proximity to an old sow, who was domiciled close by in the farmyard. I limped up to the little boys, patted their round, polished faces, and gave them each a biscuit, which I happened to have in my pocket. We trio were friends from that hour; but I cannot say so much for the farmer, who, on that and all future occasions, appeared grumpy, and seldom disposed to fraternise in the least degree. Probably it was the outcome of the fearful struggle then existing between his country and ours, which, as a common result, was most disastrous to his farming prospects; anyhow, he always looked " daggers ! "

The Russian mother now fetched the domestic, and to my great delight and surprise, I discovered that she spoke a little English. I afterwards found she had been living with her uncle at Berlin; he had married an American woman, and from her the girl had picked up a fairly good smattering of our language. I expressed my wish to see Miss Templar at once.

" Pardon, please, sir, she don't sleep here," was the reply.

I further express my desire by signs and in much plainer terms.

' Oh me do see, me comprehend; yea, yea, me do see," interrupted the girl; and turning to her mistress, she said something in their own language, and then continued,

—"The captain he do say he do want have sight, dat is, he want to look upon the Lady Red Cross."

The girl and the Russian mother held another short colloquy in the most earnest manner, during which time I was "nowhere," not understanding their lingo; but I evidently showed signs of impatience, having visions of Curtis returning. The woman beckoned me to follow her, notwithstanding a stentorian grunt from the farmer in the corner, which was unquestionably suggestive of disapproval.

After traversing two or three intricate passages, bumping the top of my cranium against sundry beams, and climbing up some dilapidated steps, which creaked on every tread, we came to a rough-looking door dotted over with large iron nut-headed nails. The woman paused, placed her ear close to the key-hole, and listened atten-

tively for a few seconds; then making a
signal for me to remain where I was, she
quietly lifted the latch, and on tip - toe
entered the room alone.   Returning in a
few moments, she took my hand and led
me to the bedside of the invalid.

It would be an effort to find words to
express the force of my feelings at this
moment.   Pillowed on a scanty bedstead
lay the brunette I had seen in my room
but a short time since.   How changed ! and
yet how exquisitely beautiful, with her
wealth of black hair falling loosely in circles
and semi-circles over a spotless breast, and
terminating promiscuously on the lily-white
sheet ; her symmetrical arm, naked to the
shoulder, was coiled around her head as if
to support it ; her dark hazel. hollow eyes
had lost much of their brilliant flash, the
light that animated them but a short time
since had toned down under the pressure of

a fevered brain, to a somewhat vacant stare;
her finely - cut lips, parched with burning
heat, were parted, displaying a set of the
whitest and most regular teeth, which seemed
to light up her pallid, Grecian face, the
lines of which were well defined; and notwithstanding her illness, and its direful
ravages on her poor frame, she was nevertheless beautiful to behold!

"This is Constance Templar," I said to
myself, "of whom I have read and heard
so much; who has earned for herself on the
battlefield and in hospital so much esteem
and notoriety, now stricken almost to death.
Fate has so ordained it, that the little hand
which fed me day and night should, for a
while, lie helpless at her side, whilst mine
is growing hourly more vigorous."

I involuntarily pressed her almost trans-
parent fingers, and felt the life blood tingle
through my veins. I breathed a vow—a

solemn vow; it was—no matter what; in heaven, I have no doubt, it was registered!

"How are you, Miss Templar?" I ventured very softly, still holding her hand in mine.

That hand!

A sudden flicker of brilliancy lit up her eyes; a flush of crimson suffused a small patch on either side of her face; she smiled —but in a moment all was "straight and cold again."

That smile!

"Don't you think you are a trifle better?" I continued, hardly for the moment knowing what I said, at the same time placing a flower which I had in my coat on her pillow.

"Who spoke? Curtis?—is that you, Curtis?"

"No; it is I."

"Who's I?" replied Constance, disengaging her tiny hand from mine, and with it shading the light, that she may discern more clearly.

" Have you forgotten me, Miss Templar ?" I continued.

" Forgotten whom ? " doubtfully.

" Your patient."

" Patient," replied Constance, " patient ! What patient ? I have had so many, that it is hard to call events to my mind. Are you the little drummer of the —th ? "

(" Not likely," I soliloquise, " considering that I am more than six feet in my stockings.")

" No, Miss Templar," I replied ; " I am the person who was so fortunate as to receive your kind attention during a prolonged and dangerous illness in this farmhouse ; and I have found my way here, with this good woman, to express to you my intense gratitude for—"

" Hush," interrupted Constance, " hush ! I have now faint glimmerings of you. Yes, of course, I know you. How silly of me— dear, dear, how silly—how silly."

"God be praised!" I said, in an audible voice, "she has her senses."

The Russian mother administered some egg and brandy; and the domestic, who was also present, interpreted to me her mistress's wish that I should not talk any more to the patient just then, which piece of advice I considered thoughtful, and was preparing to leave the room, on my crutches, when the invalid, with most surprising strength, rose from her pillow, and, fixing her placid eyes on me, said,—

"Poor fellow! poor fellow!" and beckoning me to return, she whispered feebly; "to-morrow, come to-morrow. I have had a strange dream. I will impart it. Mind and bring Nora with you."

"Good Lord!" I ejaculated, *sotto voce;* and gently squeezing her hand, and raising it to my lips, I left the room, with my heart, so to speak, in my throat.

Who is that man standing in the passage outside the door ?

Only Curtis !

" Sure then, I thought it was yer ghost, master, prowling about these draughty places ; faith I can hardly believe my own eyes."

" Hold your tongue," I say, " and get me some food."

" By the powers, ye will have some food presintly, that ye won't be able to digest, if ye are after following up such ' itemings ' as this."

" All right, Curtis," I replied ; " I shall not take cold."

" Bother ! ye don't know at all what ye may take away, or what ye may bring to the darling in that cupboard, or leastwise just what is left of her. God knows, 'tisn't much to look at ; and what little there is, ye'll be after tazing it, and tazing it, until there is nothing to be seen except a bright little speck a long, long way up somewhere above those flying clouds."

"God forbid," I murmured, at the same time greatly admiring the honest disposition of the man before me.

The various colloquies between Curtis and myself may not unreasonably strike the reader as somewhat improbable, and bring to his or her mind the well-known maxim, that one used, by way of exercise, to record in one's copying book in early days, "Nimia familiaritatis contemptum parit," which, as a rule, one should not ignore; but my relations with the faithful Irishman have been brought about under such very exceptional circumstances, that I have not the heart to take him down a "peg," seeing how he struggled day and night to lift me up many pegs, and how far he succeeded in landing me "high and dry" on the shores of health, so I let him have the full swing of his tether. The fellow, in his own way, is a strange composition, and by no means scrupulous in what he says, though his judgment is sound, his intentions are good, his heart is faithful. He has no motive in the background other than affection for me; and should I be spared, he shall surely have his reward, for, if I don't go to the front again, I will buy him out, and he and his Tipperary consort shall find an asylum for life in one of our lodges at home.

" Now tell me, Curtis," I said, letting my weak body down as carefully as I could into an antiquated arm-chair, covered with dimity, " how fares ' Rob Roy ' ? Are his wounds healing to your satisfaction ? "

" I thought how it would be. Ye just can't breathe a bit, and ye are gasping away as if it were the last morsel of air that's been dealt out to ye; and the perspiration, like peas, is cropping all out on yer forehead like the steam on the windows of Mother

Blarney's cook shop at Woolwich; and yer legs seem as if they didn't belong to ye, and are terrified out of their viry senses, for they are shivering and shaking like evermore!"

"Any letters?" I interrupt, not wishing to continue the conversation.

"Faith, a pile of them in mail bag, sir, and no mistake."

"Bravo!" I reply. "By-the-bye, have you heard, Curtis, from your people since you have been here?"

"People! did ye say, master? I have but one blessed soul upon the face of the earth that's got a thought for Mike Curtis, and that is the Tipperary girl who took advantage of me one fine morning, and asked me if I had anything to part with; and I said to her, yer honour, 'Well, nothing, Biddy, worth having.' 'Haven't ye now?' she said. 'Sure, then, I haven't,' I replied. 'You don't mane it?' she con-

tinued, putting her arm round my neck
with the greatest possible affection. 'What
are ye after, ye little monkey?' 'Well,'
she said, 'I'm just come down from the
hills to ask ye, before ye go and put yourself up as a target to be shot at, to leave
me a wee bit of something.' 'Sure, then,
Biddy,' I said, 'name what ye will, and if
it belongs to me, and sure my own property,
ye shall have it all.' 'No, Mike,' she said,
with hot tears in her eyes, 'it isn't all that
I want, 'tis only a half.' 'Out with it,
Biddy,' I replied, 'and don't ye be after
tazing me so.' 'Well,' says she, again putting
both arms round my neck, 'if you will just
give me half yer name, and take the best
half yerself away with ye, ye will niver
regret it as long as ye live, for whilst ye
are in distant lands in the wars, no harm
shall ever come to yer name, anyhow, this
side of the wather, for Biddy Flanagan is

as true as the finest gold, and, sure then,
don't ye know it, Mike?' I couldn't
doubt her words, yer honour; her pretty
face and coral lips, and breath like the
fresh air on the mountain side, cheeks like
scarlet runners, and teeth as white as the
fox hounds in Squire Sweeny's kennels, did
the trick, sure enough; faith I couldn't refuse
her at all, at all; so I just caught her up
in my arms, sealed the bargain in a very
modest way upon her lips, put a life stamp,
as I call it, on the little document, and
registered it in heaven."

"Well," I said inquiringly; "go on, Curtis."

"I just sent for Father O'Connor, sir, and
sure then we both relieved ourselves of all our
impirfictions; and Biddy Flanagan, bless her!
relieved me of just one half of my name."

A pause.

"Proceed," I interrupted; "let me have
the whole of the story."

"Twelve winters, yer honour, and twelve summers have passed away, and my Biddy, my rose of old Ireland, my shamrock of Tipperary, kept her word, and Heaven knows that Mike Curtis has kept his; and though tarnation big stones have rolled now and then in our path, and blackthorns have sprung up in our way, we have got over them, and we love each other now dearer than ever; and we both bless and riverance the day that Father O'Connor cut my name in a half."

Another full stop.

"I am charmed, Curtis, with your graphic description of the past and present; may your future, my good fellow, partake of the fragrance of the same lovely spring flowers that you culled in early life," I said, forgetting for the moment to whom I was speaking.

"I am not 'up,' yer honour, in flowery language, but I am 'up,' to many things though, as ye know. I am up to 'snuff,' and 'up' to doing a tiny bit of good when I can get the chance, and I am 'up' to give ye this advice, yer honour, if I may be allowed most respictfully to offer it; it is this :—if ye hever marry that blessed Nora that I've heard ye talk so much about in yer sleep, or the Daisy darling lying in yon chamber, just come to me, and, if you won't despise poor Mike's advice, I'll tell ye a thing or two that clenched our happiness, —that pickled it in the very best of pickles, and made it keep!"

"All right, old fellow," I said complacently ; "run downstairs now and get my dinner in an hour, during which time I wish to be quiet."

Although we had entirely (by my wish) dropped "shop" since my illness, Mike pulled himself together, saluted me, then "right about turn," "left wheel," and he marched down the back stairs, humming the tune of—

"The girl I left behind me."

CHAPTER VI.

CARTHEWIN CASTLE.

If travellers hailing from the north take train at Gloucester, or those from the south *via* Bristol, New Passage, cross the Severn to Portskewet, and from thence book for the primitive little village of ——, they will, on arriving at their destination, find themselves within two miles of Carthewin Castle, a tall turreted castellated building, formerly the residence of the traditional Macdonnell family of chivalrous renown, who maintained the fame of their ancestors, and whose descendants, so late as the present generation, endeavoured (conjointly with the lamented

Earl of ——) to revive the tournament, in which, however, they signally failed, very much to the disappointment of a large number of young noblemen and squires of notoriety, who were prepared to throw their heart, soul, and wealth into the pastime, and, in a modified form, at the flourish of clarions and trumpets, array such a goodly host of knights-errant, and others, as ever bore lance point fair against the shield and crest of opposing forces.

Carthewin Castle and manor have long since passed into other hands ; in 1740 it was sold by private contract to one Percy St Clare Townsend, a gentleman then full of years, and who did not long survive the purchase. He, however, left issue, and the present owner (of whom we shall have to speak) is the grandson, in direct line ; his name is Godfrey Townsend. He married twice ; by his first wife he had one daughter,

Nora—now living; by his second wife, one daughter, Gertrude, their ages being twenty-two and fourteen years respectively.

It will be well, perhaps, for the present, not to dilate in great minuteness on the personal attractions of Nora and Gertrude, as in giving a description in detail, it is quite possible that one or the other of those fair daughters of England may unintentionally be placed slightly in the shade. Suffice it to say that they are two beautiful girls,—the elder is stepping on the borders of womanhood, and already feeling the sunshine of bright and happy prospects, also the effect produced by the gathering of some of life's dark clouds, that have been and are still hovering over her. She is of a highly-sensitive disposition, which, united with remarkable talent and grace of manner, simple demeanour and unaffected *bonhomie* always make her a special favourite.

The younger is of tender years;—like a

rosebud, just opening and spreading its tinted leaves before the warmth of a summer's morn ; the rude tempest has not yet nipped a leaf; no cold nights have robbed it of its beauty and fragrance ; it is yet under culture, un-folding more and more, advancing step by step, by careful manipulation, to maturity. Who will pluck it ?—nourish it when gathered, and protect it from the wild blast of the world ? Echo answers—Who ?

Of the virtues of these twain—" bloom and bud "—let silence for once be the character-istic feature, until events, past, present, and future, are recorded,—words spoken in love and anger are revealed ; and actions, which speak louder than any words, leave their sure and certain mark behind ; then, and not until then, will the reader have a clear perception of the love, charity, virtue, and shortcomings of the two half-sisters, Nora and Gertrude.

Just one passing tribute to the memory of

Nora's mother. She was a lady born and bred; of the most refined taste; endowed with inestimable virtues; of a gentle and forbearing disposition, and a mind susceptible of the most elevated and generous impressions, with a pious and sensitive heart. She loved her husband with all the tenderness of her fond nature; her hopes were centred in her only child, who was the pride of her life; and last, but not least, in the strictest sense of the word, she loved her neighbour. But a black east wind, "many and many a year ago," chilled the parent flower; the keen blast withered the stalk, killing the root; it drooped, and bent its head submissively to the Divine will; the leaves fell one by one, but they left a fragrance behind that will hang around the scenes of her loving memory,—the little offshoot, with its blossom, was separated from the standard. That blossom is Nora, the heroine of our tale.

Mr Townsend remained single for seven years; but when his child began to grow up, his stringent resolution as to celibacy relaxed by degrees, and he ultimately became enamoured of a lady in Cumberland, one Julia Rodway, daughter of a rich banker, to whom he was married, it is said, with some precipitation. Her jointure being large, she brought increased wealth to coffers already well filled, and in course of time presented her husband with a daughter, of whom we have already spoken.

There is nothing particular to be said, by way of preliminary, of Godfrey .Townsend, except that he is deserving the appellation commonly given, of being

> " A fine old English gentleman,
>   One of the olden time,"

a kind-hearted, genial, easy-going country squire, with eight thousand broad acres surrounding his noble domain. He has been a thorough fox-hunting man in his early days, and always ignored "doing" the lanes, when rattling good fences had to be negotiated. He rode clever Irish horses, that could "top" exorbitant walls and big fences in a banking country in fine form and fashion; he was a capital shot, and, what is more, a keen sportsman; and, in his day, a steady bat and good oar. He entertained his friends hospitably, and always relished the society of men who spoke the truth, lived correctly; and who hated anything approaching humbug. His manners were refined and courteous. Through life he had mingled with the world in all its facial attractions, and felt its pleasures, excitement, and dangers. He was never known to suffer his steward to put the "screw," so to speak, upon any of his poorer tenants. If, from accident, or through any unforeseen circumstance, they couldn't, with a long family, make a "do" of it, he came personally to the rescue, found the rusty nail that was choking the mill, extracted it, repaired the internal arrangements, oiled the wheels, set the mill again in motion, and made many hearts glad. He was a staunch friend to the poor widow,—a prop to the fatherless,—a refuge for the oppressed; his friendship lasting, and his counsel sought for and valued. Such, in the abstract, is the character of Nora's father. Whether it was sound judgment to venture upon a second marriage, and thus mix the family of children, or, in other words, the "brood," is a matter which will probably be disclosed in the forthcoming pages; though one must not disregard the old aphorism and philosophical household words, that "all things that happen are for the best." This, however, requires qualifying, and to which should be added,—Provided we endeavour to do what is right.

·   ·   ·   ·   ·   ·   ·   ·

The trees are in leaf, the shrubs are in flower, and the birds are in song: it is the middle of May. The green slopes in the home park, stretching away for two or three miles, intersected here and there with a wide drive or footpath, are covered with rich pasturage. The silent deer, in small herds, are dotted about over the land; at the sound of noise, or any unusual sight, they lightly tread, and with a jaunty air move slowly and majestically on, following the stag; as the noise increases, or the strange object draws near, they bound away together, and fly up over the sideland, like "chaff before the wind."

Carthewin Castle stands on a promontory half way up the park; it is surrounded by a wide terrace, and approached by three lodge entrances of the most remote architecture, and from the south side, through an avenue of cedars of Lebanon; on the northern boundary, at some distance, are rocks,

precipices, brakes, and thickets, which ter-
minate in a wild mountainous country, knee
deep in gorse and heather, with here and
there a well-trodden path or rugged defile.

The sun rises with great glory over the
vast domain, and throws his brilliant rays
into the east rooms of Carthewin Castle long
before the inmates are stirring; higher and
higher he rises over the giant elms and oaks
in the park, throwing gaunt shadows on the
green sward beneath, where the deer are
nipping off the young grass, which is bathed
in dew, and the fawns are gaily sporting
with each other in the early sunshine.

The notes of the blackbird and thrush are
heard almost in every direction. The cry
of the curlew sounds in the distance, and
the lambs are careering on the green knolls.
The pretty swallow is skimming overhead,
and with graceful sweep, scoops the air, now
poised, as it were, high up, then fluttering

in a promiscuous kind of way, and darting on all sides, he is soon out of sight; others are homeward bound, industriously engaged in making endless journeys to some favourite spot, where suitable building materials are to be found for the erection of their granite-like dwellings. What lessons of industry they teach! how cruel to destroy their little homesteads, those exquisite pieces of architecture and fruits of so much labour.

Later in the day, in the quaint old library of Carthewin Castle were seated the lord of the manor and his consort. The former was taking a cursory glance at the contents of some dusty book he had found on the top range; but now and then he paused, and in a careless kind of way turned over the leaves, not reading a single line. A person of quick discernment would arrive at the conclusion that his attention was much divided — in other words, that he was considerably lost

in thought.   His spouse was seated on a
low lounging chair, with several rich velvet
cushions pillowed luxuriously at her back,
and her feet were resting on an embroidered
footstool, by the side of which were curled
up two French poodle dogs (*très blancs*),
their tiny heads resting on their paws, whilst
their round, limpid black eyes took in every
movement in the room with considerable
accuracy ; dogs, no doubt, think unutterable
things sometimes, and not unfrequently carry
out their thoughts by way of sympathy or
otherwise.

Mrs Townsend was busily engaged " casting
on " some wool knitting ; her attention, too,
was divided.   She was trying to count the
stitches in a restless manner, but for the life
of her she could not arrive at a satisfactory
conclusion.

" Things are come now to a pretty pass,
upon my word," said Mrs Townsend, trying

another count, and drawing herself up with an elevated demeanour.

Poodle number one wagged his tail approvingly.

"Can't you make it right, Julia?" said her husband, carelessly looking over his gold spectacles.

"I am not speaking of my work, Godfrey."

"What, then, love?" affectionately.

"Your daughter, sir."

"Our daughter, you mean, dear," significantly.

"Indeed, I do not; I have never taken upon myself that immense responsibility, Mr T.; and at my time of life, and delicate state of health, it is hardly likely that I am going to try the experiment at this juncture."

"Juncture!—what juncture?"

"Climax, if you prefer it," continued Mrs Townsend, trying another count.

"Climax!—What climax?"

"Fatality, then—anything you like," snappishly.

"Fatality! Good heavens! Julia, what do—"

"Oh yes, of course, you pretend not to comprehend my meaning, Godfrey; very convenient sometimes."

"I don't, upon my soul. I—"

"Hush, Mr T. I wish you would not be so fond of talking so lightly about your soul. We cannot have a little rational conversation together on domestic matters without your introducing, in the most frivolous manner, that invisible part of you."

"Now, don't put yourself in a pet, dear. You know it makes you cough and ill for days. I will endeavour for the future to keep my soul to myself," said Mr Townsend, smiling; "but tell me, what about this 'juncture,' 'climax,' and 'fatality'?"

"Have you seen your daughter this morning?" said Mrs Townsend, at the same time winding off some wool with great rapidity.

"I have not had that pleasure yet," replied Mr Townsend. "I am afraid she is seriously indisposed; indeed, I know the announcement of the death of poor Snowdon has been a crushing blow to her."

"Crushing fiddlesticks!" interrupted Mrs Townsend. "Crushing blow, indeed!"

"In the midst of it all," continued Godfrey, "I feel for Nora with all my heart; and if I had ever dreamt of young Snowdon turning out such a noble and brave fellow on the battlefield, I would never have withheld my sanction to their marriage; he should have had Nora, he should, upon my so—"

"There you are again, with your soul," interrupted Mrs Townsend warmly; "fie upon you!"

"Pardon me, Julia, I feel strongly in this matter, and therefore, perhaps, speak somewhat hastily."

" And indiscreetly, Godfrey."

" Probably I do; but you must make allowances for a father's feelings."

" Yes, Godfrey," replied Mrs Townsend, with evident signs of temper, " and there are very considerable allowances to be made for a mother's feelings; but that, of course, does not for a moment occur to you."

" Julia," said Mr Townsend, taking off his spectacles, and slipping them leisurely into a tortoise-shell case, which he closed with some emphasis, " let us, as man and wife, reason together.   Difficulties have, no doubt, been created through a little indiscretion on the part of Nora; but to ' err is human,' and the very best of us fall short of the landmarks that are placed for our guidance.   Her present sorrow, the cup of which is running over, is known only to her poor heart: it has sprung up in a brief season; her sensitive nature has yielded to the withering blow, struck by a mighty hand. Let us go, dear, to the rescue ; like the father who met his prodigal son, let us, as far as we can, endeavour to bind up the broken heart, first of all removing the worm that is preying upon it."

" But she absolutely refuses to come near us, Godfrey,—locks herself in her boudoir, and will see none of the household but her maid, who, in all matters, is ridiculously reticent : it is simply monstrous ! "

" The bird, Julia, that is wounded will naturally flutter and limp away to the first hedgerow, and will there conceal the damage it has received, suffering in loneliness, whils its life-blood is slowly ebbing away."

" It is no use talking," replied Mrs Townsend ; " I have not common patience with Nora. First of all she had no right, without our sanction, to form an attachment with a young man of such small pretensions, and one

who was not, strictly speaking, a 'county'
man,—whose pedigree, as far as I can ascertain, cannot be traced back, with any degree
of certainty, beyond his grandfather; and
his mother's antecedents, judging from what
I heard the other day at Lady Bole's, are
very questionable indeed. To think that your
Nora—the lovely and accomplished Nora, as
you designate her—should have so far de-
scended in the scale of society as to dama
our name by the introduction of a person
of somewhat obscure origin into our circle,
is really most provoking and heartrending."

"Not likely in your case," said Mr Townsend, *sotto voce.*

"Did you speak, Mr T. ?"

"No, dear, at least nothing of importance,"
was the meek rejoinder.

"I don't relish that mumbling to yourself, Godfrey : that vague way you have of
apostrophising words is most objectionable ;

I prefer hearing in a loud and audible voice what you have to say; in short, I positively detest such smothering of language; it is not kind to keep from me anything that is in your heart."

"Years ago, Julia, I gave you all that was there. You then thought that an exchange of hearts, so to speak, would not be altogether amiss. You promised to be a fond mother to my Nora; she was to be your child, as well as mine. Her every reasonable desire you undertook to grant; her education to superintend; her general training to cultivate; and, in fine, to launch the motherless child in the world, as an ornament to society. How far you have acted up to those solemn promises, you best know."

"I have been a good wife to you, Godfrey, and a good mother to our daughter Gertrude," said Mrs Townsend, aspiring to tears,

in which piece of performance, both poodles
contributed and sympathised immensely.

"You have been, I grant, fond and true,"
continued Mr Townsend, "and I trust I know
how to value a heart that is, and has been,
wholly mine. I am not unmindful, Julia, of
all your goodness, or insensible of my debt
of gratitude; and if there have been any
shortcomings on your part in the attention
which I reasonably looked for as due to
Nora, it is partly counterbalanced by your
unbounded and undying love for our daughter
Gertrude ; but," continued Mr Townsend,
walking over to his wife, and placing his
hand affectionately on her shoulder, "remember, Julia, in the chancel of yonder
church, under that white marble monument
which we look upon every Sabbath, there
lies the mother of my Nora, the fond parent
who adored her child,—who clung to the
little offshoot even in the agony of death,—

entwined her infant hands around her neck, and then, with eyes beaming with love and admiration for her suckling, she handed the charge upon trust to me, with these words,— ' Take her, thine own, Godfrey. God in His benignity has considered it wise to separate the branch from the tree : it is, however, only for a short time ; the germ will not die, it will quicken again ; the sap will spring up ; and we, I trust, shall be reunited ! but in the interim that may be accorded you and our beloved offspring, for the affection you bear me, for the vows you plighted, religiously discharge your promise, by the careful culture of our beloved daughter ; and God-frey, dear, let me implore you, whilst your paternal roof shelters our child, the object of my most earnest solicitation, whilst you temper your love with the seeds of indulgence and your correction with duty, sow them, Godfrey, by way of example, in good ground,

that our daughter, as she grows into womanhood, may see the fruits of your work, and
reap a rich reward from them. Above all,
be "Firm as a Rock !"' Those," continued
Mr Townsend, in a solemn voice, "were
my lamented and ever-beloved wife's last
words," and burying his massive head in
both hands, he left the room.

CHAPTER VII.

OUR HEROINE.

" She is far from the land where her young hero sleeps,
    And lovers around her are sighing ;
But coldly she turns from their gaze, and weeps,
    For her heart in his grave is lying.

She sings the wild songs of her dear native plains,
    Every note which he loved awaking ;
Ah ! little they think who delight in her strains,
    How the heart of the minstrel is breaking.

He had lived for his love, for his country he died,
    These were all that to life had entwined him ;
Nor soon shall the tears of his country be dried,
    Nor long will his love stay behind him."
                                    Moore.

SPRING, in all its beauty, has now fully appeared. The dark and russet - brown branches of the oak, elm, and ash have put on their summer clothing; the buds have unfolded into leaf; the orchards and kitchen gardens are gay with the richest blossoms, which, at every rude gust of wind, throw off a shower of variegated leaves which cumber the ground; privet and common hedgerows are thickly set; holly berries, that have fed so many birds through a dreary winter, have now well - nigh disappeared; ivy berries have changed colour, and are ripening fast; large pink and white May trees stand boldly forth, here and there, and seem to vie with each other for supremacy. There are old feelings, old associations, happy reminiscences of our childhood entwined, as it were, around the branches of those May trees. Perhaps we have sported under their shadow; have climbed to their limbs and summit, at the cost of many a severe scratch and tumble; have culled from the hard-wooded branchlet pretty bits for a mother, sister, or lover; and we have enjoyed their sweet fragrance in the gloaming of a summer's eve, when the gentle breeze carried with it an odorous perfume, which spoke its own language, denoting the time of year, the bright and happy season, opening in all its loveliness and elegance before us !

The birds, too, with their wild, delicious notes, pour forth brilliant renderings of sweet summer's song, answering each other from the lilac bush to the orchard, the orchard to the meadow, the meadow to the shrubbery, the shrubbery to the park, where the high notes of our beautiful songster, the thrush, as he lifts his little beak towards heaven, arrests the traveller's attention, awakening the soul of the lover of nature to a keen sense of the supreme work of the Creator, as he listens and enjoys the amenity of the wild songs of the birds,—admires the gay clothing of the trees,—the rich verdure on which he is treading,—the ultramarine vault above, with its silvery clouds floating silently overhead; and the broad, glassy trout stream beneath, on the bosom of which majestically sail before the wind the lady of the lake and her consort, those beautiful white swans, decked out in the richest of plumage. All this is lovely to behold : such sounds are charming to the ear; such sights delightful to the eye, and food for the mind. It wants no enthusiastic soaring of the imagination to contemplate this supreme work : it is before us in all its glorious reality; and one cannot but pity the unfortunate individual whose soul falls short of realising its splendour!

It was a delightful evening, with such surroundings as described, that a beautiful girl, draped in the deepest crape, sauntered along the banks of the glassy lake. The young May moon, with pale-faced crescent, faintly beamed on the dusky form that glided noiselessly across the sward; the birds were singing their *dulce domum*, ever so sweetly; the lambs in the meadow were skipping blithely round their mothers, whose long fleeces of wool denoted the approaching season for shearing.

But who is this beautiful girl in black, with the pensive countenance, pallid face, and golden hair flowing over her craped shoulders, gazing so abstractedly on the shadows of the huge trees, as they swayed to and fro? It is Nora, the heiress of Carthewin Castle. Draw closer, friendly reader, nearer and nearer to her heart and thoughts. She is lonely and sad, for—

"Her heart for her minstrel is breaking."

"Happy couple," soliloquised Nora, as her eyes dreamily followed the swans, who gracefully breasted the stream towards her, stretching forth their crane-like necks in the hope of receiving the usual broken biscuit from her gentle hand. "Happiness itself," said she; "would that I could take at this moment such spotless plumage as thine, and glide away with you twain on these peaceful waters, and so get rid of the tearing pains of anguish I am enduring. It seems but yesterday, dear birds, that my lamented Percy enticingly stretched forth his hand to feed you. Little did I think that the 'crumbs of comfort' which you eagerly took were to be his last offering. Oft in the summer's eve, in the gloaming, have we traversed these paths together. It was here, by this cooling stream, we plighted our love; it was here we invoked Heaven to grant us our desire, and make us one. The dark clouds parted in the firmament, the sun smiled upon us, the atmosphere cleared, the summer looked gay, the birds were in song, and oh, how happy we were! But the new moon came, and with it dense clouds ; and then I walked these banks alone—my noble boy, my beloved ——, and yet not my ——, went to the wars ; darkness truly has set in on the early morn of my life, on the spring-tide of my womanhood, and left me sad and desolate."

" Desolate ! " said a deep-toned voice, that seemed to echo through the colonnade of trees, " desolate ! dost say, girl ? " continued the lord of the soil, who had crept up unobserved ; " come, come, I'll have none of this ; desolation is unknown whilst the owner of Carthewin Castle and his fair daughters' voices can ring in the hall of our forefathers ; come, come, Nora, throw dull sorrow away, tear the veil of grief from thy sad heart."

" My beloved father," sobbed Nora, " my heart will surely break."

" Your mind, my child, can be read on

your brow. I know all about your trouble, Nora, and from my very soul I sympathise with you, because I feel that I have helped to bring it about, by allowing Snowdon to go to the Crimea ; but have courage, child, have courage."

" You don't know all about my trouble, dear father, and it is impossible for you to sympathise with me, utterly impossible. I must bear that grief to myself: it is of my own seeking. The thunderbolt has struck the child of disobedience, and the lightning of God's vengeance has rent my heart in twain."

" That is precisely what He does, Nora, to the children of disobedience, to humble them before He binds up the broken heart again," said Mr Townsend, gently placing his arm around his sobbing child's neck.

" My own dear father," gasped Nora, resting her head on his broad manly breast, and raising her liquid blue eyes full in his face in the most pitiful manner.

"Come, come, my daughter, what ails thee? Have done, have done, or thy mother's spirit will come from her grave to us."

"Hush, dear father," said the trembling girl, timidly looking around in all directions, "speak that name beneath the breath; I have offered an indignity to her memory; I have not adhered to her written injunctions, —that letter containing a stream of never-ending love. Her affectionate warning, her anxiety for me, has been ignored; all of which I should have treasured up in my mind as a beacon wherein I could find shelter when no other counsel was near. Oh, how richly do I deserve the pain and sorrow which I now endure! Had you listened to my earnest pleadings, father, I—"

"Be calm, my daughter, be calm; it is

never too late to mend.   Your voice, your
language, your very look denote reparation.
The fountain of your heart is flowing in the
right direction.   I breathe more freely.   I
have you still, my own dear child, by my
side, unsullied, untouched by the rough
hand of time, and in all your youthful
simplicity.   Look into my face, show me
those features where the reflex of thy
lamented mother is portrayed in all its
grace and beauty."

Nora tore herself from her father's embrace,
stepped from him two or three paces, pressed
back with both hands the waving wealth of
hair that had fallen promiscuously over her
face, and said vehemently,—

"I cannot, I dare not receive another
caress until I have told you all; yes, all,
dear father.   I am undeserving the confidence
you reposed in me; I must hasten from your
presence until a suitable opportunity presents

itself for disclosing to you, sir, how far I have forfeited your love and esteem."

There was a bewildering pause. A shudder ran through the bulky frame of Godfrey Townsend as the last words fell from the quivering lips of his daughter. The shrill, well-remembered voice of his termagant wife rang out the words, as it were, "juncture!" "climax!" and "fatality!" The blood rushed to his face and back again to his heart with mighty force, leaving a countenance deadly pale. The soft rays from the young moon fell faintly on father and child as they stood gazing tearfully at each other in distressing silence.

Nora was about to fly from her parent's presence, when he intercepted her, and drawing himself up with an elevated demeanour, he pointed to the turreted castle and battlements that stood out in bold relief under the woodland, and said,—

" Listen to me, Nora, listen to what I have to say. Mark well, and inwardly digest. In yonder walls, from time out of mind, our people have lived and brought up their children with credit and distinction ; not one dark spot has ever stained the escutcheon of our family ; and if a blemish is to sully our fair name, then truly your father's grey hairs will go down in sorrow to the grave. Speak, child, I implore you."

Nora appeared riveted to the earth, and, with hands clasped, was lost in silent reverie. She listened to the solemn words of her father ; she was a witness to his disturbed state of mind. She realised her position in all its intensity, and felt that the " juncture," the " climax," and the " fatality " had arrived with a vengeance. Now, or never, must the secret be disclosed.

There was another long pause. Not a sound could be heard except the delicious notes of the black-cap warbler on a distant bough of a tree, who poured forth from his little throat a shower of diamonds that echoed through the valley of the park.

"Say on, Nora, say on; I am impatient; I am prepared for the worst," said Mr Townsend, tattooing the ground with his foot in an excited state.

"Lord give me strength!" murmured Nora, placing her hand upon her heart, which was violently beating. "Father, dear father, I— I—I—"

"I what?" shouted Mr Townsend.

"I—I—I—"

"I what?" again interrupted her father vehemently.

"I—I am a widow!"

"A widow! Nora?" dubiously.

"Yes, sir, a widow!" impressively.

"Oh! is that all?"

"All? I do not comprehend you," rejoined Nora, sobbing loudly.

"Only married?" continued Mr Townsend, evidently greatly relieved.

"Married, sir, and yet not married," timidly.

"Legally, Nora?"

"Legally."

"Where?" said Mr Townsend eagerly.

"At the registrar's office."

"When?" anxiously.

"Ten minutes before. we parted for ever."

"God be praised it is no worse!" ejaculated Mr Townsend. "I comprehend it all."

Then—father and child were locked in each other's arms.

.   .   .   .

The weight of trouble that had pressed so heavily on Nora's heart is lifted; the secret known only to herself and a lady friend is disclosed. The fond parent whose heart thumped so loudly against the pale face of

the " Virgin Widow," has not, in the hour
of intense grief, turned from her with the
ominous word—Begone ! He is still the tree
of her life, so to speak, whose branches she
can cling to, whose shelter she can seek when
the blasts of the world drive her to look for
repose under its boughs ; or when the clouds
of adversity, sickness, or sorrow shall gather
around her, she can climb to its centre, and
nestle there as in days of yore !

Poor Nora, she had no mother to counsel
her !—no fond parent, at that sure and certain
age of life when the young mind, green as
the twig just cut, can be bent to any
shape ; like the ivy that promiscuously forces
its way through an aperture in the wall, can
be trained by a careful hand and watchful
eye in the way it should go. Though Nora's
governess, a lady of rank and high attainments,
had brought her acquirements to bear upon
her pupil, yet the fringe only of her gentle

nature could be touched, the heart could not be reached, and its inmost recesses searched and purified by any other person with the same precision and results as by the tender manipulation of a mother, who can, in most cases, mysteriously define the way her off-spring should go ; whilst a stranger, however estimable, talented, virtuous, and loving she may be, will fall considerably short of the mark.

So it was with the Honourable Mrs Mac-kenzie, who had the conduct of Nora's ad-vancement. This lady seemed charged with determination, and with the important duty of educating her pupil to opera pitch ; or, in other words, to the highest pressure. It was study, study, from Monday morning until Saturday night,—the same old story over and over again, with little intermission or recreation. At last it became exceedingly painful : the constant "cramming" surfeited Nora's young mind. As the morning dawned, instead of bringing with it sunshine, happiness, health, and spirits, the days seemed irksome. She longed for other scenes, for the sunny side of life, for a heart she could call her own, and her flesh cried aloud for rescue.

When Nora was seven years of age, her stepmother cast her anchor within the walls of Carthewin Castle,—a lady, be it said, of considerable talent and personal attractions, who was always looked upon in Cumberland as a thorough "blue stocking," and who, at one time, was likely to remain true to her maiden name for the rest of her days. Though on her preferment, and in the prime of her life, none of her relations or friends ever dreamt of her (using a homely phrase) "settling" in life. Her nephews and nieces adored their maiden Aunt Julia: she was such a "jolly good soul." They never went to see her without a ten-pound note was quietly slipped into some pocket, which was conveniently left open for the occasion ; or the folds of the dress so arranged that there was not much difficulty in finding a safe repository for " sovereign remedies ! "

Apropos of marriage, ladies not unfrequently change their minds, and they have, undoubtedly, a right so to do. At one time, Julia did not altogether believe in men : she considered them vain, selfish creatures, and abominable deceivers ; there was only one dear soul on the face of the earth, in her estimation, who was worth a " rag," and that was her father, Cuthbert Rodway, old " Ready Money," as the people used in vulgar parlance to call him, a kind of sobriquet which he rather liked than otherwise, for he was never known to be annoyed with anyone for taking such familiarity. But the said father could not live for ever, and in the usual course of events, in the affluxion of

time, he departed this life, full of years,
greatly respected, and much beloved! at
least history so records it on piles of black-
edged cards, which were freely circulated at
the time. Legatees too, placed their hands
significantly on their hearts, and spoke in
the highest and most endearing terms of
the lamented Mr R., and the "reward that
was surely his." There was another class,
too, that spoke freely and unreservedly, some
disappointed "loafers," whose pockets are
turned inside out, as an emblem of dissatis-
faction; this very "select circle" are rather
sceptical as to the whereabouts or repose of
the soul of old "Ready Money;" they shake
their heads ominously, and express their
views freely that things would, no doubt,
have been better with the late proprietor of
"Rodway Hall," had he remembered them
in a corner of his will!

Nevertheless Cuthbert Rodway was a good

man in the eyes of the world! He was a fond parent, an excellent friend, and good to the poor; therefore, peace to his memory!

At the death of her father, Julia, with a quarter of a million of the current coin of the realm, began to revolve in her mind as to whether there could not be found in the county a thoroughly reliable, presentable, and, in every sense, advantageous suitor. So Julia, in course of time, just at that period when it was "becoming," the "correct thing," and the usual formalities had been scrupulously complied with, by placing aside deep crape for half mourning, and finally slight ditto, she availed herself of the approaching Easter season, and again reappeared in the most *recherché* costume, direct from the distinguished firm of Misses Robealls, of Regent Street, who had obtained great notoriety for close fit, ease, and elegance! Customers had only to apply to that firm, personally, and they could be re-, juveniled to a most extrordinary extent. Money being no object, Julia (prompted inwardly by a desire to cut the acquaintance of celibacy at the earliest possible moment consistent with the conventionalities of society) went " in " extensively for the counterfeit method of being made " beautiful for ever," and it was not the fault of the house of the Misses Robealls if the brilliant and artful display of costume they brought to bear, did not earn for Julia Rodway considerable reputation as a lady of beauty and leading fashion !

In time, garden parties were organised with gorgeous display, great variety of entertainment, and marked selection of " circle," which, it is needless to add, were all " county." A new archery club was instituted, to be held periodically in the picturesque grounds of Rodway Hall, under the immediate control of Julia, at which place assembled all the " big " people (so-called) of the neighbourhood.

At one of these garden entertainments or greensward soirees given by Julia Rodway, appeared the lord of the manor of Carthewin, and his lovely little daughter Nora, who was then a child of seven years. It is needless to add that the handsome widower and the late rich banker's daughter thought it advisable to form an alliance. The lady claimed for herself great attainments, and her wealth was undisputed; added to which, she was in possession of her fair share of other adornments in the way of good looks; but had Godfrey Townsend, like a far-seeing and sensible man (as he had the credit of being), sent some good and pious sister to spend just one month with his *fiancée* they never would have married. Those sisters ! how clever they are ! How they can pry, dive, dig, uproot, sift, and weed ; indeed, where a brother's interest and future happiness are concerned, no one so fit as a sister to discover weak points, facial disposition, and evil tempers, thereby not unfrequently arresting at an early stage, matches which may prove to be unequal, unsound, ill-assorted, and fraught with many dangerous breakers ahead.

CHAPTER VIII.

I GET INTO SAD DISGRACE.

Our surgeon managed, during rather an easy time at headquarters, to gallop over to the farm. He pronounced me to be very much better, though by no means (in camp phraseology) "fit," except to go home on leave, for I had a deep sabre wound that refused to heal to the doctor's satisfaction, much less to my own; nevertheless I felt that I was picking up my "crumbs," and that my general health was mending apace, notwithstanding the doctors disagreed on the subject. Such being the present position of matters, I most reluctantly gave up all hope and thought of going again to the front, and have determined, at the earliest possible moment consistent with prudence, to bid good-day to my Russian landlady and her precious surroundings, and embark with Curtis and "Rob Roy" for England, to my father's seat in Gloucestershire.

But there is just the slightest attraction here, a magnetic influence, which I can only express by saying that—

"I feel just here, but I cannot tell how."

Now I have intimated before in this narrative that such a thing as loving a girl, other than with a brotherly love for my sister, never for one moment entered my head, neither have I the vanity to suppose that any of England's fair daughters ever cared a "straw" for me ; notwithstanding, I felt an inclination to sojourn for a while in these quarters. I also had a desire to get home, and by way of an attempt to make a clean breast of it, I will simply say,—

That picture!

That brunette!

It is a trite saying that "a wheel cannot run in two ruts, nor a man keep opposite sets of intimates;" but how true it is that expectation will darken to disappointment, disappointment to anxiety, anxiety to despair, but the renewal of hope will generally revive all, and give consolation, and the man who abides with unshrinking firmness the bitterest blasts that fall upon our poor frail nature, may indeed be said to have achieved much worth possessing.

Around my neck is suspended in a circle of gold (or, as poor Percy called it, the "Shadow in the Gold") a likeness of certainly one of the fairest and most beautiful girls that eyes ever looked upon. If it be a faithful representation of Nora, she must be intensely exquisite, and her graceful figure the most charming to behold. One is carried back to some words in the Irish melodies,—

" O my Norah Crena dear,
    My mild, my bashful Norah Crena ;
Beauty lies in woman's eyes,
    But love in yours, my Norah Crena."

" How extraordinary," I soliloquise, " that my friend Percy should have invested me with this miniature portrait,—decorated me with all that was dear to him, requesting me to see the original,—to deliver that Bible, the marker too, and to repeat his dying words.   Then again, that sealed letter, addressed to " Nora," Carthewin Castle, South Wales, which he charged me to post immediately after his death.   Heaven and the dear girl only know its contents.   I shall have little peace of mind until I visit Carthewin Castle and discharge the duty entrusted to me.   How vividly I call to remembrance those long chats with Percy, which not unfrequently ran into the small hours of the morning, the prevailing conversation being Nora, Nora; if we branched off to other subjects, back he came with increased vehemence to the old and favourite story. Somehow I seldom if ever grew tired of listening I loved the brave fellow, and felt an increasing pleasure in loving anything that he loved, disliking whatever he disliked, and opposing whatever he opposed. I had confidence in him, and he in me. Long travel, and the closest intimacy, brought out the reflex of our hearts, and exhibited to each other, as in a mirror, that which was passing within;—also the nature, value, and durability of our friendship, which time had cemented more and more closely.

Yes, as soon as my health will admit, I must contrive to see this lovely girl,—look, if only but once, upon the idol of my lamented friend. The little creature haunts

me day and night; yea, verily, when my
eyes were closed in sleep she appeared to
me in a dream more like an angel in heaven,
with tears of affection for her slaughtered
lover coursing one another down her pallid
cheeks. She came, and, as it were, leant over
me, spoke not, but looked unutterable things,
and then smiled sadly—that smile!—combed
her long wealth of hair between her tiny
fingers, pointed to the book-marker and then
to heaven, showed me a wound in her breast,
and vanished from my bedside.

That dream!

> " In slumbers, I prythee, how is it,
>   That souls are oft taking the air,
>   And paying each other a visit,
>   Whilst bodies are Heaven knows where?"

But, God willing, I will see the original,
and, if I can help, in the most disinterested
way, to heal the wound that must be preying
on Nora's heart, I will religiously do so.

Whatever may have been the inward thoughts and wishes (to say nothing of the outward manifestations) of my dear friend, as to my future, in connection with his Nora, it is idle to conjecture. I will offer no indignity to his memory by seeking his beloved with any feelings charged with aught save the purest friendship; to do otherwise would be to draw upon her affection by discounting the materials I have at my command. No; I will dismiss from my thoughts all that is past, and leave the future in higher hands. It shall never be recorded that Oliver Grey made "capital" out of the dying words of his friend.

> "The path of sorrow, and that path alone,
>   Leads to the land where sorrow is unknown."

As yet I have disclosed but a brief outline of the thoughts that are passing through my mind. In yonder woods, leaning on the arm of her servant, is Constance Templar, taking an airing. She has so far recovered as to admit of venturing for a walk, but she has hardly strength to drag her poor bones in the sunshine, and is manifestly making desperate efforts to pull through the tedious illness from which she has barely escaped with her life. How I long to run up and put my hand forth to help her, and enjoy a *tête-à-tête*, but the little creature has grown of late so confoundedly reserved that it is with difficulty I can induce her to hold more than a few minutes' conversation with me; she invariably has some important letter to write, which will admit of no delay, or the cold blast from the mountain is too much for her—she must return to the farm; and down go those black eyelashes fringed on her cheeks as she glides from my presence, leaving me simply "nowhere!" But never was there a more benevolent heart, or a more simple, sincere disposition. Dear girl! how she watched over me, how earnestly she attended to my wants, which she considered to be her duty; but it was all for the "red cross." Now her work is at an end,—she is pining for other scenes of labour: I, of course, am nothing to her. She may be nothing to me, but there are springs of the heart that will not easily dry up; and so long as Constance Templar lives, so long I shall consider that I owe a debt of gratitude not sufficiently repaid. I feel that were I like many other men in disposition, I should be very quickly "coquetting" with her, and serenading the little brunette in the most endearing manner. But there is nothing of the sort about me; in other words, I am lamentably deficient of self-esteem, and the peculiar material requisite for such gushing display, and should certainly break down at the last moment and let another fellow pluck the flower, whilst I am dreamily enjoying its fragrance in the distance!

And thus I continued thinking as I sauntered into the back room, where, when night comes on, I rest my weary bones on a rickety bedstead. Not being in the best of spirits to-day, I paced my dormitory in mute reverie, and flattened my nose against one of the panes of glass, contemplated the active scene that was going on in the farmyard over which my room looks. There was a Muscovy duck and another quarrelling over their liquor (as Washington Irving has it); judging from the oscillation of their tails, they were in high dudgeon. Yes, there was the old sow, too, that had for the last month been sounding the loud timbrel early and late under my window, and filling my room with villainous perfumes, wafted from her bijou residence. Looking over a dilapidated stone fence was the " wall-eyed " roan cob that carried the proprietor of the farm twice a day round the estate. By no means the least interesting scene was the serenad-

ing of the sultan, that game cock. Verily
he is a nobleman, every inch of him. His
pedigree is considered good ; he is a paragon
of a bird ; just watch him. See his wealth
of plumage ; note his politeness, as with elevated head he approaches his consorts, who,
manifestly, look up to and place the most
absolute confidence in his spurs and protec-
tion! Like a knight-errant of old, who led
a roguish, roving kind of life, wooed and won
many a fair lady by his lance and spurs.
Should our feathered sultan find a termagant
wife in his harem, how gently he chides her,
and how soon he makes it up again by
manipulating endless little acts of kindness
in his own way. See how anxious he is over
their bodily welfare, how particular not to
allow his wives to quarrel with one another.
He is obviously philosopher enough to know
that "a house divided against itself cannot
stand." What valuable lessons they teach

us! Watch them as they come out of their
tiny shells; follow them from incubation to
maturity; note their actions; see their indulgent mothers training their young in the
way they should go!

I take one, just one, more hasty look at
" Dandy Jim and Caroline" in the happy
farmyard, make my own deductions, light my
pipe, and limp downstairs humming,—

" What's all this dull town to me, Robin's not here?"

.   .   .   .

On my return home, an hour later, I found
Curtis in a disturbed state of mind as to my
absence, and very anxious to make some pro-
posal, though I wished him, for the moment
at Halifax or anywhere else, having important
letters to prepare for the mail-bag, notably to
my beloved mother, and, " dear sir."

" If you please, yer honour," said my valet,
at the same time drawing his hand down his

partly bald cranium, "what do ye say this morning to a nice little drive through the forest? I am just thinking it may do ye a tiny bit of good,—take yer 'tintion away from other things, and ye just won't be brooding over matters."

"What can we drive, Curtis?" I interrupted.

"Never fear, yer honour, I have made arrangements with the farmer, who is going to lend us the wall-eyed roan colt in the orchard; and sure then, I have borrowed a rare good sledge for the occasion."

"How about my wounds, Curtis, over those atrocious roads?" I reply, shrugging my shoulder.

"Oh, bother the wounds, master; ye have had sharper work than that, sure enough, many and many a time, over a tarnation rougher country than this, and no mistake."

"All right, Curtis, order dinner at six; be

sure you see that the trappings of the harness are sound, breeching and kicking-strap
adjusted, and put the reins in the lower bar ;
one does not quite know what may happen
with these " high flying," strange Russian
horses; besides, the brute may be touched
with the same complaint as the Czar, and
may have a great horror of us English just
now, and kick over the traces."

"Sure I niver heard ye discourse about
the risks of horse flesh before in my life ; it
cannot be Captain Oliver Grey that is spaking
about danger signals, bolts, bars, and sich
like."

" To tell you the truth, Curtis," I replied,
" I am not altogether in the best of ' fiddle,'
physically, or otherwise, to deal with strange
tempers, and raw colts are ticklish ' customers.' "

" Niver fear, master, I'll manage it all to
yer intire satisfaction, and make a fine bed

of roses for ye to lie on.   But ye will excuse my being so bold, wouldn't ye jist like,
by way of company, to ask that lonely
little black-eyed daisy darling to go with
ye for a drive ? "

"Well done, Curtis; capital thought, my
good fellow, capital thought; notwithstanding, I don't think she'll go."

"Bless ye, master, ye jist don't know
her as well as I do.   A little bird came one
evening, and sang me the prettiest song I
hiver heard in my life : it was all about the
daisy darling and yer very own self, sure."

"About me ! " I anxiously replied ; "what
on earth do you mean, Curtis ? "

"Faith then, I like to unbutton the collar
of my coat, and spake out freely all at once,
whilst I'm about it ; sure then, the little
darling has preserved the pretty flowers that
ye placed on her pillow, when we all thought
she was going to live with the cherubims,

and she has tumbled over head and ears in love with ye, anyhow."

" With me!" I exclaimed; " humbug, Curtis!"

" I niver heard it called by that name before, master, not niver."

"Who is your authority?" I asked doubtfully.

" Authority, did ye say?"

" You know perfectly well what I mean; who told you all this ridiculous nonsense?"

" A devil a bit of nonsense is there in the daisy darling, and ye may take my word for it."

" Who is the little bird, Curtis?" I ask playfully.

"Sure then, it was a charming little nighting-gal, who always sings the Irish melodies without any ' blarney.'"

It was useless my attempting any further questions on this head; nevertheless, Curtis's gratuitous information caused me to pace the room in mute and anxious delight.

"Did ye tell me to do anything, yer honour?" asked my valet, who was intently eyeing me with some astonishment.

"Yes," I replied, somewhat incoherently. "I wish you to ask—yes—of course—I wish you to—let me see—"

"Oh bother!" said Curtis, *sotto voce;* "if I don't just about think that the captain is going 'off his head,' and is taking another journey Heaven knows where."

"Did ye spake, sir, plase?"

"Yes, Curtis; execute my order, and let me know the result as soon as possible."

"Faith ye didn't give me any structions, master, and that's all the result I can offer."

I felt, for the moment, "small," my attention being divided, consequent on the new feature in my life in connection with the pretty little brunette!

"Curtis," I said, "when Miss Templar returns from her walk, go to her room;

knock quietly at her door; give her my compliments, and ask her if she will do me the honour of— No, no; simply say this, word for word,—'If you please, miss, the captain sends his kind regards, and hopes you are feeling better this morning; and he wishes to know if your health will admit of your taking a little drive this afternoon in the forest with him.' Now be sure, Curtis, you let her know that you are going to accompany us."

"Sure, master, wouldn't it be much more the 'ticket for soup' if ye went by yerselves. Yer honour will find me very much in yer way, and I may be after just hearing what I didn't ought to."

"I have nothing to say to Miss Templar, Curtis, but you or anyone else may hear."

"Fie upon ye, master! I'm ashamed of ye, sure then I am. When I was yer age, if I had suddenly found myself tucked up by the side of such a splendid polished bit of 'stuff' as that, sure then my tongue would have been too big for my mouth; and, by the holy poker, if I shouldn't a made her mouth wather, anyhow, with the fine choice things I should have to say about the honey-moon,—the splendid little home I should take her to on the Tipperary hills,—the cow and the fine pig I should buy her,—the tatee field I should till for her,—the bright prospects of a rising generation,—how good and kind I should be to her when she was ill,—how we would go together to mass every week, and confession every new moon, and unburden our hearts, and get rid of our imperfictions, and start fresh; and, above all, yer honour, how I would love her ten times more than ever when old age crept upon us; yes, that I would, sure!"

During this gratuitous peroration, I turned my head away to conceal my mirth. I did not dare openly to portray my feelings, or I should have run the risk of having, sooner or later, too much of a good thing, and was obliged to exercise a little *finesse* in steering clear of what we should say, in ordinary parlance, "too much familiarity breeds contempt."

"Attend to my instructions, Curtis; and let me know what Miss Templar says."

"Exactly, captain. Compliments, ye said, didn't ye? That's the only thing I'm bothered over," replied Curtis, scratching his head, a curious habit which he had when in doubt.

"No. I told you as plainly as words can express,— kind regards; now be careful and—"

"Oh, kind regards," rejoined Curtis, much perplexed.

"Yes; now be off with you, for I wish to write my letters."

"By way of variety, master, may I be so bold as to take upon myself the sponsibility of giving yer love instead of that cold-'arted thing compliments?"

"No, you idiot!" I replied, with considerable emphasis, "do as I tell you, and, for Heaven's sake, don't make a hash of it!"

"But I'd make yer honour the viry best Irish stew of it, if I only had the chance; sure the little daisy darling don't want any of yer compliments, regards, or sich like: she wouldn't know what to do with such trifling matters; but if ye send her something worth having, that she can pickle up close to her little loving heart, sure then ye never will regret it, anyhow!"

Having impressed Curtis with my full determination in the matter, and given him a quiet hint that the sooner he made tracks the better I should be pleased, I plumped down in my dimity arm-chair, filled my meerschaum, and sent endless circles and semi-circles of smoke here, there, and everywhere, and with each puff, many anxious thoughts as to the future.

The contents of the mail-bag received in the morning filled me with alarm, for the health of my beloved mother was anything but cheering ; my favourite sister's approaching marriage is spoken of ; and reference is made to my brother Stanley's " wild oats," also father's acute gout, and how much he is hypped with it.   There is, however, a " crumb of comfort " in dear sir's letter, by way of a draft for two hundred pounds, and a refreshing *P.S.* at the close, viz., " More to follow, if absolutely needed."   The word " absolutely " was scored, and in parentheses.

I felt much concerned about my mother, whose health of late has been sadly declining. How I long for home, to bask once more in the sunshine of her countenance,—listen to her loving voice, and a repetition of the sound and valuable precedents she endeavoured to establish in my young mind. Bless her! how far I have profited by them, or how I shall bring her earnest injunctions to bear on my future career, will be made manifest hereafter. Alas! many good resolutions have been made and broken in a day,—duties neglected,—promises unfulfilled,—vows plighted,—contracts bearing a solemn seal registered in a "volume of a book," and attested by a mighty witness, have been disregarded, torn asunder, and trampled, so to speak, under foot. What poor creatures we are! How the mind wanders, wavers, twists, and turns from sound ground to unsound; from deep waters to shallow; from pure streams to murky and stagnant pools; from sunshine to darkness; and from hope to despair. Notwitstanding all such varieties, and continual oscillations of our nature, there is a landmark straight ahead, standing out in bold relief. The "look-out man" can see it plainly; it only requires a well-adjusted compass, a little nicety of navigation, to reach the haven. If the good mariner run his bark before the wind, select the proper inlet, and keep clear of dangerous points that are jutting out, he will cast anchor safely under lofty battlements; but if he tack with long reaches, the chances are that he will "fetch" on a rock, and his frail ship will break up in sight of home.

The preceding are some of the meditations which not unfrequently creep into one's mind just at that uncertain hour of twilight, in the gloaming, when the shades of evening fall upon us, and press back the light of heaven. Thoughts of one's childhood, one's happy home, and one's beloved mother, are pleasant themes to dwell upon. May I continue to appreciate her goodness, and treasure up in my heart the sound maxims she inculcated, and imitate as nearly as I can her exemplary life and excellence ; but all things depend upon an infinite and incomprehensible bounty. Without it nothing can be effected or obtained, and, after it is obtained, be of any value, force, or power, without the same concurring grace.

.   .   .   .

Still revolving in my mind endless and very anxious thoughts respecting the little brunette,—the odd speech of my eccentric servant, I again take from under my waist-coat the " Shadow in the Gold." Somehow I treasure it more than anything I possess. There is a history attached to the portrait, making it of inestimable value to me. Though it contain but the shadow, the reality or sub-stance may ultimately prove a gem of price-less worth. Though I never looked upon that sweet face and graceful figure, yet there is something in the placid countenance that speaks volumes to my soul—yes, peaceful as a summer's dream.

" *Gardez,* Oliver Grey," I soliloquised; " *gardez !* Remember the trite maxim, that things done in haste are often repented of at leisure. Be watchful over your thoughts, your words, your actions ; and be discreet ; take not a single step without mature consideration ; and, above all things, don't by any indirect means work upon the feelings of the girl who sacrificed so much for your benefit, and then leave her in doubt, perplexity, and grief.

I knocked out the ashes of my meerschaum, and deposited the jewel of a picture in its old quarters, when I perceived Curtis very leisurely coming down the gravel path, brushing off some snow from his regulation boots, and finally wiping his mouth with the back of his hand. He proceeded up the winding stairs, but his step was much slower than usual; he stopped on the landing ; there was an ominous silence, suggestive of much. He was evidently thinking. I know him of old, and I intuitively felt there was something " up."

" Come in. Well, Curtis, what does Miss Templar say ? " I asked again, pulling away vigorously at my meerschaum, which I had refilled for the occasion, and blowing a cloud of smoke across the room.

" No, yer honour," dismally.

" No ! What else ? "

" Sure, captain, she must have been uncommon short of breath, for that's all the blessed word I could get out of her."

" Nonsense, man, Miss Templar never sent such a message ; I'll answer for that," pulling again at my pipe.

" Faith I don't call it a message at all, at all ; the mess of a word isn't worth looking at a minute."

"Tell me, Curtis, what is the meaning of all this?"

"Maybe, master, the little daisy darling has had a bit of a nightmare, and a d—l a bit does she want the dose repeated with a day mare, for maybe she doesn't like the look of the high-flying colt in the orchard, and maybe she—"

A gentle tap at the door.

It is Miss Templar's maid, with a note for Captain Oliver Grey.

At the sight of the caligraphy, I felt my heart make one solitary bound. I eagerly tore open the envelope, and read as follows:—

"DEAR CAPTAIN GREY,—The message your servant brought, has filled me with amazement! and I cannot but think there must be some mistake,—either that you intended it for someone else, or that your valet has become suddenly demented. If your request has been interpreted correctly, I have yet to learn that the duties of my calling, which necessitated my attending you in your sickness, are to be construed into anything other than the faithful discharge of a responsibility I religiously undertook,—a vocation entrusted to me, and which has always filled me with delight ; but, happily, I know how to protect my spotless name from anything like tarnish, and it is well I am so fortified, seeing in what an atmosphere one occasionally breathes. —Yours faithfully, CONSTANCE TEMPLAR."

" Sure then, captain, ye are getting some more thumping red potatees in yer face, anyhow ; what is the matter with ye ? "

" Matter with me, you rascal," I said, dropping the letter on the table with positive fright ; " tell me instantly what message you delivered to the lady ! "

" What lady, yer honour ? "

" Why, Miss Templar."

" Oh! the daisy darling, ye mean; sure then, I gave her a very tidy missage, and one which I thought would make her little mouth wather."

" What did you say, you old idiot?" I gasped.

" I said, yer honour, what ye told me."

" Will you swear you did not add to it?"

" My memory isn't over clear, master, jist now. I know I told her what ye told me."

" Your memory isn't clear, is it? Now, look here, Curtis," I said, tucking up the sleeves of my coat, "much as I like you when you are sensible, and weak as I am, if you don't refresh your memory instanter, I'll break every bone in your body."

" Sure, then, ye will be after a-sarving me like the thaif on the cross, and sure I am not desarving so much attintion from ye, anyhow."

" Out with it, you old fool," I interrupted, pretending to make a grab at his collar, " or I'll send you to the front with the forlorn hope to be shot, as sure as eggs are eggs."

" Well, yer honour," replied Curtis, with great *sang froid,* " as sure as there is bread in nine loaves, I'll be after telling ye the whole epistle and gospel, chapter and verse; but ye must take yer hand from my collar, and release my throat, or the Irish blood that my respicted father and mother gave me may go from simmering to boiling, and maybe it will boil over and scald one of the very best of creatures that ever lived, and Mike Curtis, of Tipperary renown, forget himself, whilst the red-hot poker is stirring up live coal under him."

The poor fellow was right. In my hasty temper I had sadly forgotten myself, and I am sure my friendly reader will make considerable allowance for impetuosity, seeing how choleric he made me. I released my hold of his throat, folded my arms, and walked to the other end of the room, saying,—

"I am sorry, Curtis, for displaying so much temper; but come, let us be rational, give me word for word the message you delivered to Miss Templar."

"Well, yer honour, now that ye have anchored your tongue, and put into the cradle your weak, spider-like arms, I'll just about accommodate ye. I saw the daisy darling hanging on the arm of her maid in the woods yonder, limping along like a duck with a wounded leg. Well, I says to myself, Mike, now is yer time, lad, to deliver the message, so I took the pipe that I was smoking out of my mouth, and cleared my throat of all obstructions, prepared myself generally for the occasion, and walked up to the stile, where I saw the darling, very weak, yer honour, so I just said to her, in my very softest manner,—'Maybe ye'll let me lift ye over, my dear;' and she tightened herself straight as a poplar tree, and asked me if I knew to whom I was speaking, and her bright eyes flashed like fire at me; so I thought, captain, I had made a bit of a mistake somewhere, and that I would rectify it at the earliest moment, so I says, 'God be praised, it is the good nurse of the Red Cross I am speaking to, my own dear master's binifactor; and, please, miss, the captain sent his compliments and very best love to—' "

" D—" I said vehemently.

" What did ye say, master? Fie upon ye! fie upon ye! and not a father-confessor in the neighbourhood either."

"Go on," I say, " you—"

"Ye bother me so, I don't know quite where I left off. Oh, now, I recollect. I said,—'Master sends his compliments and very best love, and to ask ye to go for a drive with him into the forest.' So she began to tighten herself again like a steel ramrod, and two scarlet runners climbed into her cheeks; and the maid that was with her caught the same complaint, tossing her head about also; and they both looked 'daggers' at me."

"Well," I gasped; "what did she say?"

"She shrugged her shoulders, threw her eyes aloft like a dying duck in a thunderstorm, lifted her hands like Father O'Connor when he gives us a blessing, and said, 'Go back to yer master, and tell him, No.'"

"I don't want to hear any more, Curtis, that is quite enough," I replied, pacing up and down the room.

" Sure, then, she never gave me another word to tell ye, anyhow."

" I should think not; you have finished it, and can now retire as soon as you like."

Curtis instantly made tracks, and I am left again to my own reflections to heal, by some potent means, and by prompt action, the wound that my thick - headed nondescript has innocently given to the feelings of a lady to whom I am so much indebted.

I light my pipe again, as the best thing to do at this juncture, the narcotic fumes of which generally have a tendency to enable me to solve a difficult problem. I re-read Miss Templar's caustic letter with anything but complacency: her high dudgeon is conspicuous in every line. I arrive at this conclusion, and am more than ever convinced that the representative of the " Red Cross " is one of the right sort.

CHAPTER IX.

I EXTRICATE MYSELF FROM THE DIFFICULTY.

I REVOLVED in my mind the whole difficulty in which I was placed with the Red Cross nurse, through the stupidity of my servant Curtis, and determined to go down and have a personal interview with Miss Templar, in the hope of putting matters straight. It may appear somewhat odd, during the last few weeks, that Miss Templar and I have not met; but it is explained by the fact of her persistently keeping so much to her room, and for some reason showing manifest symptoms of aversion to encounter me. If at any time the brunette, *en route* to the garden, heard my step in the hall or on the stairs,

she would rush off at the " double " and hide
herself, like a discreet bird in the hedgerow
in a thunder-storm. Being a sensitive man,
and a keen observer, I was alive in a moment
to anything like standoffishness, so in time
I somehow seemed to have caught the same
complaint, and invariably made " tracks "
when I should have gone on. How quick
girls are, as a rule, to observe ; how well
they know when a man is " putting it on ;"
how easily, and with surprising certainty,
they discriminate the difference between that
which is facial and that which is real, and
occasionally decipher one's countenance, and
arrive at a fairly correct conclusion as to
whether one's actions are really the outcome
of good and honest thoughts or not.

Yes, I must see Miss Templar without
further delay. Apostrophising a word or
two—something like " Bother!" "Great nuis-
ance ! "—I make an attempt to hum a merry

tune, but lamentably failed. Probably Miss Templar may think that I have some sinister motive. How I hate motives. I mean those ignominious chess-like moves that people not unfrequently take in their journey through this life, checkmating their neighbour, thereby putting in pawn, so to speak, what should otherwise be our noblest thoughts and best actions, which sometimes we are never in a position to redeem.

Having made up my mind as to the course I should pursue, I walked down the back stairs to Miss Templar's room, *via* the larder. Pausing at the latter, I took out the " Shadow in the Gold," had a hasty peep at the jewel it contained, and said within myself,—" *Gardez*, Oliver ; *gardez!* "

I made a full stop at Miss Templar's door. Good Lord ! how my heart thumped. I could face a storm of shot and shell from the Russian batteries without flinching or turning a hair ; but the thought of the brunette's caustic remarks in her letter took all the " fight " completely out of me, and the wind out of my sails.

I knocked at the door ; oh, such a humble knock !—so gentle—just such as one would probably give at a dentist's establishment when requiring his services, and yet at the same time *not requiring* them, if I may so express it, heartily hoping that Messrs Dragum & Tearum may be anywhere but at home. Who hasn't felt at some time of his life a sense of false relief, when told by an apple-faced youth in bright buttons that his master could not be seen until ten o'clock the following morning. Anyway, the writer owns to that cowardly feeling. But I digress.

" Come in."

Miss Templar was intently reading the *Times ;* and on my entering, thinking probably it was the domestic, she did not trouble to look up, neither did her maid, who sat by her side, vigorously plying her needle, though evidently in deep thought. I cleared my throat—the usual preliminary of a nervous man—Miss Templar then calmly lifted her eyes with the greatest *sang-froid*. What an absence of excitement, I thought. As for the maid, she did something spasmodic, as though an apparition had appeared from heaven knows where. Her young mistress looked at her with astonishment, and drawing herself up with a lofty air, said,—

"Has anything happened, Clara ?"

"The captain, miss," was the meek rejoinder, pointing to me.

The girl was about to leave the room ; but I detected Miss Templar making a vigorous motion for her to remain, and the maid subsided again into her low-backed chair, settling down to her work with increased industry, every now and again looking askance at her mistress.

"How do you do, Captain Grey?" said the Red Cross nurse, recovering herself, and walking across the room to meet me, holding out her thin white hand in the most friendly manner; and, with some enthusiasm, continued, "I am so glad to see that your health is rapidly mending. Pray take a chair."

"It is very kind of you to say so, Miss Templar," I replied; "and I am greatly indebted for all the attention you paid this poor wounded, fever - stricken soldier on the—"

"Pardon my interrupting you, Captain Grey. I make a point of never receiving any thanks or acknowledgment for services rendered,—duties which have been entrusted to me, and which I endeavoured to discharge unostentatiously and creditably. Should I not, I trust my patients will report me at headquarters. One thing is certain, I exercise the same amount of zeal, and feel as much interest in a drummer or gunner as I should in a general."

"In returning you my thanks, Miss Templar, I am simply discharging the obligations I owe to your kind favour."

"It is there," rejoined Miss Templar, "that you fall into error. Pray believe me sincere when I assure you that you need not for one moment consider yourself under any obligation for services rendered by me. If you have very strong feelings of gratitude —which you naturally would experience in common with all convalescents — you know exactly where to make acknowledgments for endless mercies vouchsafed unto you," at the same time pointing her finger towards heaven, and throwing her beautiful dark hazel eyes, with the longest of lashes, full in my face.

Those eyes!

"I feel, Miss Templar, that I have yet another duty to perform, and were I not to discharge it, I should be wanting in courtesy and sincerity; therefore, notwithstanding your protest, I thank you most heartily for all your goodness and your untiring energy day and night, when my life seemed to hang upon a thread, and quivered in the balance, so to speak, between this world and the next."

"You will, I am sure, Captain Grey, pardon my observation, but permit me to say that I think you are mistaken. At the very worst time of your illness you were a very long way from the entrance to that long valley to which you refer. There is no such thing as chance in these matters. True, you were brought apparently to death's door, but the portal was closed. The great God of all creation works out the map of our lives on sound and good principles of

His own; we know nothing of the measure or scale, but on the chart there are clearly laid down warnings of sunken rocks, head-lands, and other indications of danger and obstruction; lighthouses and lightships too are jotted down to guide the mariner on his perilous voyage. Your illness, Captain Grey, depend upon it, was one of those blessings which come to us in disguise; the result will, no doubt, make itself clearly manifest in due course, and you may rejoice some day, when you look back on the hours of anguish you spent in this lonely farm-house, and contemplate with infinite joy the warning voice that reached you when your frail bark was tossing about in mid - channel and in imminent peril of foundering."

"Blue stocking, for a hundred," I thought.

"Yes, Miss Templar," I stammered, "I shall contemplate with infinite gratitude how I have been rescued, and the mercies vouch-

safed to me by the Giver of all good gifts;
and I shall also remember, with feelings of
inexpressible joy, the oar you so religiously
pulled in helping my frail boat to land
safely,"—at the same time wishing myself
anywhere else but in front of the brunette,
who was cutting me nicely into ribbons, or,
in other words, paddling me very considerably out of my depth; I therefore thought
it best to turn the subject, by continuing,—
"I must ask you, Miss Templar, to kindly
excuse my paying you a visit at this early
hour."

"Pray don't offer any apology, Captain
Grey," replied the Red Cross nurse, playing
with a bunch of charms attached to her
waistband, and evidently anticipating what
was about to follow.

"I was going to observe, Miss Templar,
that my visit here at this unreasonable hour
has a threefold object."

Miss Templar bent her head inquiringly, and smiled complacently.

" First and foremost, in spite of your protest, to thank you for your goodness to me in sickness. Secondly, I come to say how rejoiced I am to find that kind Providence has permitted you to be restored to health ; and lastly, to put right one of the most absurd blunders that was ever made by a stupid servant."

"Oh—exactly—yes ; I presume you refer to your Irish nondescript," replied Miss Templar, considerably scrutinising my features for some indication of what may be passing in my mind.

" You could not think me guilty, Miss Templar, of offering you an indignity ? "

" Pardon me, Captain Grey, my knowledge of you, and all your brave, noble, and generous actions in the camp and on the field, is such that I am quite sure you could

not be guilty of offering an indignity to anyone, much less to a lonely woman in a foreign
country. I must confess I wrote you that
letter somewhat in haste : it was the outcome
of a disposition made extremely irritable by
protracted illness ; but looking at my position, the course I adopted was the only one
open to me—don't you think so ? "

"Well, to tell you the truth, Miss Templar," I replied, evidently warming to my
work, " I certainly thought you rather
' down ' upon me. The contents of your
letter greatly alarmed me, and it was very
nearly the means of having my servant
pitched out of the window, for, in my haste,
I was that way inclined ; and I think I should
have enforced the extreme measure, but the
fellow, just as I was about to commence
operations, told me word for word what
transpired ; and it is needless for me to say
that a great portion of the thoughtless mes-

sage he gave you as coming from me was purely his own invention, and may be attributed to a freedom of speech which the lower class of Irishmen not unfrequently indulge in."

"Good, kind Curtis," said Miss Templar. "I have a very clear perception of the susceptibilities of Irishmen, having mixed so much with them in hospitals. Your servant is, undoubtedly, an oddity; but I have a great respect for the man. Upon further reflection, do you not think that I acted perfectly right in sending you that letter?"

"Well, Miss Templar, you will pardon my saying so, but I am afraid we must agree to differ."

"Ah, I see," said Miss Templar, pinking up very considerably, "you are sceptical; you pause over admitting the prudence of the stern epistle I wrote you. Well, well, let us reason together for a few moments,

and consider, as far as we can, how matters
stand, and how far I acted prudently. We
will suppose, by way of illustration, and
bringing the case nearer to your domestic
circle, that you had a sister,— one you dearly
loved, one in whom you placed the most
implicit confidence, one who had given up
the gaieties of life for a season, for such an
arena as you find me at this moment engaged
in, and in which I have been working (I
hope zealously) for some considerable time ;
or we will imagine, by way of striking, perhaps, more closely home, you were affianced
to a young lady whose inclination led her to
pursue the vocation I have the honour and
privilege of following ; and we will further
suppose that your *fiancée*, in the discharge of the duties entrusted to her, had
to attend to some dashing wounded officer
through a long and trying illness ; he re-
covers, but during the progress of recovery

he is stimulated, either by a sense of gratitude or otherwise, to make overtures beyond
the bounds of courtesy, limits of custom, or,
in other words, conventionalities of society.
The meek-hearted, guileless sister, or *fiancée*,
as the case may be, at first mistakes the
approaches of her convalescent: her mind
may be too pure to have anything like a
clear perception of the motive in the background; until the man, emboldened by apparent advantages he has obtained, tears a
portion of the veil from his heart, so to speak,
and exposes some of the dark mixture with
which it is charged! What then would you
say of your sister, or coming bride, were she
to resent a familiarity with all the force of
her chaste nature?"

"What should I say, Miss Templar," I
replied, with some degree of earnestness;
"why, just one word."

"May I ask what that one word would

be ?" rejoined the brunette, tattooing her little foot impatiently on the floor.

" Jewel !" I replied.

" May such a ' jewel,' Captain Grey, be yours, and may your daughter, should you ever have one, reap the benefit of the prisms that such a lustrous brilliant would reflect."

"The mighty force of your observations, Miss Templar, admits of no doubt whatever. Every word you have uttered has conveyed to my mind a soundness which is the characteristic feature of a well-trained—"

" Suppose we now change the subject to matters more agreeable," interrupted Miss Templar, evidently fearing that I was about to say something immensely " gushing ; " and I am not quite sure that I was not going to make a fool of myself, but the presence of Miss Templar's maid, who was ensconced in one corner of the room stitching away like mad, was very provoking.

"I am rejoiced to see," went on the Red Cross nurse, that in the last despatches sent home by General —— your services have been prominently noticed, and in due season you will undoubtedly have your reward for the distinction so nobly and dearly earned."

"All scraps, Miss Templar, most thankfully received," I replied ; " but, alas ! there were brave comrades far more deserving than myself, now 'slumbering on earth's cold pillow,' who, had they been spared, would have shared those honours with me."

"Yes," replied Constance Templar, " such are the fortunes and misfortunes of those engaged in this horrible struggle, when hosts against hosts are arrayed in a mighty conflict, such as we are now experiencing ; but to those fond relations who have lost a member of their family in the discharge of his duty, it must be eminently consoling to know that he distinguished himself."

At this juncture I should have brought our *tête-à-tête* to a close, but Miss Templar gave me another of her extraordinary searching looks, at the same time pointing to the locket which I had stupidly managed in my excitement to drag out of my pocket, and which was dangling at the side of my waistcoat.

" You will lose your pretty picture, if you don't take care," said Miss Templar significantly.

Good Lord! how I coloured. Miss Templar noticed my embarrassment, and the rubicund tint. I am quite sure she made a mental note of it, for one of her subdued smiles lit up her beautiful face, and there was a playfulness about her manner, somewhat suggestive of pleasure, · but which I could not at the moment exactly decipher. The precious locket had flown open, and exposed the ivory painting of Nora.

" I hope, Captain Grey," said Miss Templar, with the sweetest expression, "I shall not appear inquisitive if I ask whether that picture in the locket is the reflex of the lady who so much occupied your delirious thoughts during those long nights I watched over you?"

Up went the colour to my face and neck again, and I stammered out something to the effect that "I was not aware of having exhibited any manifestations respecting the young lady whose image that portrait re-presented, particularly as I never had the pleasure of seeing her."

"Never seen her?" dubiously.

"Never, Miss Templar, on my honour," vehemently.

"Surely, then, you saw her plainly in your imagination, and conversed freely and tenderly with her," jocosely.

"Good heavens!" I said, very *sotto voce*, but recovering myself, and, with well-forced *sang-froid,* I continued,—"What on earth I could have to say about a person I never saw, is certainly a riddle to me, and I am rather curious to know."

Miss Templar folded her long white fingers within each other, sceptically shook that wonderfully powerful and thoughtful head of hers, and said,—

"A greater riddle to me to see a gentleman wearing a locket containing the likeness of a lady he has never seen ; but I trust I do not appear the least inquisitive."

"Not at all, Miss Templar, not at all ; there is an old saying, 'In for a penny, in for a pound,' and now that we are by degrees getting up the ladder, perhaps you will obligingly tell me, miss " (I laid the stress on miss), " what I had to say about the lady in question ? "

"No, indeed ! I would much rather not," replied the Red Cross nurse decisively ; " those matters are profound secrets which nurses never disclose."

" Well, just the name, please ? " I asked playfully.

" No ! " seriously, and down went those long lashes on her cheeks.

" You say ' No,' Miss Templar. I presume that that is but a moiety of the name. As we have got as far as ' No,' suppose I add the other half, and submit ' ra,' will that answer to the name, or come anywhere near the mark ? "

" Precisely, Captain Grey, and most ingeniously you have arrived at the truth ; yet you tell me (though not without signs of embarrassment) that you have never seen the lady ; how very curious ! "

" Well, it may seem strange, nevertheless it is an absolute fact. I shall shortly be homeward bound, Miss Templar, and hope, on my arrival, to have that pleasure accorded me, and surrender to the lady this picture, which was given to me by my lamented friend and comrade-in-arms, Lieutenant Percival Snowdon, on his deathbed."

"Good heavens! you don't speak it!" exclaimed Miss Templar. " What! one of the heroes of 'Slaughter Hill'?—the brave Snowdon of so much notoriety?"

" Even so, Miss Templar."

" Do let me look at it, Captain Grey,—just one look at that face."

I detached the locket from my chain and handed it to Constance Templar, with, I am ashamed to say, a trembling hand.

She gazed at it for several moments in silence, and then said sorrowfully,—

" Yes, it is, it is—how much like her most excellent father. There are old associations connected with my people and the Townsends of Carthewin Castle, also the Rodways of Rodway Hall, in Cumberland, that fill me with intense emotion."

"How extraordinary," I replied, "that you should have known Miss Townsend."

Miss Templar gave me another searching look, as she replied,—

"I cannot say I know much of Nora. I met her at Rodway Hall many years since. Poor girl! her horizon was that of romance, and she has paid the penalty; yes, poor girl, I have no doubt that is a correct picture,

> Though very small,
> Much like her shadow on the wall.

Ah me!" went on Miss Templar, with slow articulation, "in so short a time, too—a bride—a wife—a widow, and—"

"A mother," I gasped, hardly knowing what I said.

"Oh, dear no," replied Miss Templar, evidently pitying my ignorance, and showing no disposition to enlighten me on a subject which I would have given one of my eyes, so to speak, at that moment to have been made acquainted with.

"I am obliged, Miss Templar, for according me this prolonged interview. I trust I have not bored you?"

"Not at all, Captain Grey, your visit has afforded me infinite pleasure, and I shall look forward to meeting you in dear old England, when we shall be able to compare notes, and look back with feelings of intense gratitude for being rescued from a furious fever that assailed us both; by then, I hope you will have recovered from the wounds that I know are still troubling you."

"God bless and protect you for all your kindness," I replied, and taking her hand in mine, I respectfully bent low and pressed it to my lips.

"How unemotional she is," I thought, as with measured steps I left the room.

CHAPTER X.

OUR HEROINE'S STEP-SISTER.

Pensive and sad the maiden wandered
   Down by the deep translucent stream;
Where her lover so oft had pondered
   O'er his happy young life's dream.

There, beneath the old oak spreading
   His wealth of branches of verdant green,
Knelt the lonely maiden, shedding
   Tears where her gallant boy had been.

IMMEDIATELY after Nora's most sensational interview with her father was over, she hastened home, went straight to her boudoir, where, throwing herself on her knees, she thanked the Giver of all good gifts for his tender mercy vouchsafed to her.

How rejoiced she was when she found that

her only earthly prop was still by her side to lean upon,—that he had not turned from, rejected, and despised her in the hour of crushing sorrow. She reviewed every word that had been uttered down by the lake,—her father's temporary agony as he listened to the disclosure of her secret,—his amiability and forbearance; one event after another kept crowding in rapid succession upon her bewildered brain; but the prevailing grief was still preying upon her heart; uppermost it would rise in spite of everything, and pour forth breathings of lamentation into her very soul.

Who has not, at some period of life, had a trouble that outweighed every other, which seemed to wrestle and grapple with every pleasure that presented itself to the mind, and in one fell swoop cleared the brain of all joy and happiness? But hope, that sweet restorer, that everlasting harbinger of peace, comes to the rescue, and we live in repose again for a brief season. Alas! how brief; for too frequently the same vexatious trouble is ready at any moment to spring on the first gleam of happiness that forces its way into our hearts, throwing a damp, dark mantle over the bright prospects of our lives!

There is only one way of disposing of the evil consequences attending the frequent presence of such an enemy, and that is, to strike a well-tempered axe at the root of the evil. It has been said by a learned man, that the true physician first purifies the blood before he attacks the tumour; so, in like manner, let us endeavour to be careful of the trashy seed that we are constantly (and very often innocently) dropping into our nature, from which the rankest weeds and the bitterest herbs spring up, and in their wild growth entangle our limbs, ensnare our bodies, entrap our minds, engross and warp our best thoughts, and cumber our pathway through life with serious obstacles.

In our heroine's case, no one is more alive to the fact of the false step she has taken, and for which disobedience and violation of her parents' injunctions she is now bowed down with sorrow. In an unguarded moment she yielded to the earnest solicitation of her lamented lover; she became his bride after considerable persuasion; she precipitated a clandestine marriage, fearing that her father and Mrs Townsend (who had threatened her with a convent life if she persisted in receiving the attentions of Lieutenant Snowdon) would take steps, when her lover left for the Crimea, to separate them for ever. But Nora's mind was so pure, so free from guile, that nothing on earth would ever have induced her to consummate the marriage until her Percy returned from the war, and they were reunited openly in Carthewin church, where her mother's remains are deposited.

In order that the course of action which they pursued should not hereafter be subject to misconstruction, or liable to get tarnished with suspicion by idle rumours and uncharitable remarks, it was so arranged that in the registrar's office they should separate, and separate they did, alas! for ever.

Nora sat at her chamber window watching the rising of the young May moon, which shed her pale light on the pallid features of the sorrow-stricken girl as she gazed vacantly over the noble domain in front of her, and the long streak of mountainous country that stretched away in the distance as far as the eye could reach. The stars sparkled brightly in the firmament; the huge sons of the forest, those majestic oaks, elms, and cedars spreading their wealth of branches in all directions, stood out in bold relief, round and about the

park, and threw their long, curiously-shaped
shadows on the greensward beneath, verily
fitting monuments of Nora's illustrious ancestors; the deer are silently browsing on the
slopes; the white owl, with his beautiful
plumage, noiselessly pursues his course from
the roof of the thatched barn to the granary,
then round the castle, at intervals passing
the casements, as it were to take an occasional
peep at the fair-haired, lonely girl; the bats
are flitting here and there; the whispering
brook that supplies the moat at the base
of the battlements with the pure mountain
stream, speaks its own sweet language as it
falls down precipitous places, carrying with
it pebble after pebble over mimic waterfalls,
meandering its way through circuitous routes.
Oh what melody!—what peace!—what repose,
to a mind stricken with grief!

Since the death of Nora's lamented husband, the "Virgin Widow" sought such

secluded scenes as the manor and its wild surroundings afforded. From dawn to meridian she wandered on the banks of the glassy lake, climbed the rugged defiles of the mountain, or picked her way through the entangled underbrush of the coverts and growth of laurel and seringo, mechanically appearing at the castle at luncheon time, eating with haste and apparent relish, and then to her rounds again until sunset, when she would get her light guitar, seek her lily-white swans on the lake, and beneath the shadow of the umbrageous trees sit down on the moss-covered bank, and sing—

He's far, far away, o'er the bright silvery cloud,
   It is there that his banner is flying;
His body's at rest, with a cloak for his shroud,
   On the banks of Crimea it's lying.

The same pale-faced moon that is beaming on me,
   O'er the grave of my hero is shining;
But the voice of thy Nora shall warble to thee,
   For the heart of thy lover is dying.

Nora thought of all her father's goodness,—how he promised he would support
her in the hour of trial ; but she was not
so sure of her step-mother, who, she felt
satisfied, would view things in quite a
different light to Mr Townsend.   There
would, in all probability, be an everlasting
outstanding grievance, having, by her pre-
cipitate and clandestine marriage, cast a dark
shadow over the prospects of her step-sister.
She knew, alas ! too well, that the termagant lady, having now something to handle,
would use the powerful lever she had at
command to humble her, and thus bring
about a scheme for a separation from her
father and her paternal roof.   She felt, as
long as she remained at the castle, there
was nothing left looming in the future but
years of inexorable dulness and detestable
bickerings.   She knew, too, how particularly desirous Mrs Townsend was to affiance

her to her (Mrs T.'s) nephew, Cuthbert
Rodway, a gentleman of moderate fortune,
and J.P., a member of a very old county
family, presentable enough, but he is reported
to be of reckless habits and vicious temper.
It is needless to add that the very sight
of such a man, to a sensitive, chaste girl
like our heroine, was most offensive, and
made her choleric, when she would have
otherwise been gentle and forbearing; hence
many little family domestic feuds sprang up
when Cuthbert Rodway's name was introduced. It is not, therefore, to be wondered
at that such lugubrious surroundings pressed
heavily, and made sad havoc in the mind of
Nora, driving her to the secluded retreats of
her father's domain, where she could enjoy
undisturbed the amenity of the wild songs
of the birds,—watch the spring flowers un-
folding, day by day, to the season,—gather
some truant bees that wandered far from

home, and got caught in the evening, and, with her gentle hand, restore them to their homestead; and listen to the murmuring brook telling its little tale, so to speak, of pleasure and sadness.

As before stated, our pale-faced heroine sat in her boudoir, looking over the moonlight scene in silent reverie, meditating on the past and anticipating the future, when a gentle knock is heard at her door.

" Come in."

" Oh, Gertrude, is that you?" said Nora, at the same time brushing away some gathering tears, and hastily folding a letter that was lying on her lap, in the handwriting of the late Percival Snowdon, whilst the envelope disclosed the well-known caligraphy of Oliver Grey.

Gertrude at first made no reply, but taking a chair, and placing it close to Nora, sat down, resting her head on her step-sister's shoulder, and entwining her arm round her neck, said softly,—

" Sissy, come, love, come, love, with me; you are lonely, you are sad."

Nora, gently pressing her back, and gazing thoughtfully into her sister's face, said,—

" Child, what do you know of my sadness ? What whisperings have reached your guileless ears, to make you thus feel interested in the troubled waters of my life ?"

" You have a papa, have you not ?"

" The Lord be praised, I have," responded our heroine.

" I have a papa, haven't I, Nora ?"

" You have, child, and a noble father he is."

" Your papa is my papa, is he not, Nora ?"

" Even so, dear," affectionately.

" He loves you tenderly, Nora, does he not ?"

" With all his soul," responded Nora, vehemently.

" And me ? " asked Gertrude.

" With all the force of his good nature. Yes, Gerty, he loves you as earnestly as he loves me ; but why all this ? "

" Why ? Oh, nothing, at least nothing very particular. I have only been thinking a little lately," was the meek rejoinder.

" Tell me, Gerty, what have you been thinking about ? " said Nora, entwining her snow-white arm round her sister's waist.

" Oh, nothing."

" Do say—do tell me," entreatingly.

Gertrude clasped her arms round her sister's neck, buried her face in her bosom, and sobbed aloud. Oh those loving, innocent tears, that flow from the fountain of the inmost recesses of a fond, childish heart ! What volumes they speak ! How they open up the springs of our sluggish nature, and soothe the drooping spirits !

"I do love you so, Sissy," sobbed Gertrude, with eyes suffused with tears.

"Your words and actions denote your love, my dear," replied Nora; "but, alas! I have no tears to shed,—the fount is dry, yes, dry as hay," at the same time casting a glance at the letter she held in her hand; "but go, dear, go. Your mother may wonder where you are, and—"

"Love me all the more, Sissy, for coming here to cheer you, I hope."

"But what makes you think I require cheering?" continued Nora thoughtfully.

"Oh, I have heard mamma and papa say ever so many things about you; and papa said, that if things did not alter at once, he should send you abroad: I think he said to Uncle George's at Cadiz."

"And what did Mrs Townsend say to such a sensible proposition?" asked Nora, twisting a bunch of keys rapidly between her fingers.

" Oh she—"

A pause.

" She what ? " earnestly.

" She said it was the very best place for you to go, to bring you to your senses, and that the sooner you changed your name to Rodway the better, and that she would be able to arrange and put matters right with Cuthbert."

A shudder visibly passed through Nora's frame as she replied, by way of a ruse,—

" And would you like me to change my name, child ? " searching into the very depths of her sister's countenance, to see if she had a knowledge of what had taken place.

" Don't ask me such a thing, Sissy. If you marry that horrid cousin of mine, you will be leaving me, and—"

" And what, love ? " interrupted Nora, with gentle earnestness.

"You will soon be grey," continued Gertrude.

"But I am grey."

"Nay, Sissy, only a tiny fleck, just here. I never noticed that before last Sunday, at church, and I then thought it was owing to the stained glass window. What is the cause of it, dear Nora, and you so young, too?"

"Your years, dear Gerty, are much too few; your loving heart too innocent and pure, to understand such things. As your days roll on, they will bring with them, as a common result, vanity and vexation of—"

"But mamma says," interrupted Gertrude, "that I am much beyond my years, and that I know as much as any grown-up woman."

"Would you like to be a grown-up wo-man?" asked Nora musingly, and evidently bent upon fathoming the mind of her sister.

"No, indeed, I should not."

" Why ? "

" Because grown - up persons half their time seem to be fretting and troubling about little things ; and they get sometimes angry and spiteful ; and they say so many cross words ; and never seem as happy when they get up in the morning as they do at dinner, and all that sort of thing."

" Dear child," soliloquised Nora, " how true every word. As the tide flows on, how it picks up on its way endless weeds. So with our journey through life—pleasures, griefs, hopes, fears, success, non-success, care, bereavements, and crushing blows of various kinds, all tend to disturb the tranquillity of the mind, and render us more or less subject to its influences."

" Then you would not like to be a tall lady, Gertrude ? "

" If there is one reason more than another, Sissy dear, that I should like to jump out of these short clothes into long, it would be to get clear of those horrid lessons I have to learn night after night ; and Miss Reignforth is so very exacting. Mamma insists on having me crammed with all kinds of accomplishments. You don't know how I am worried, dear, and how my poor head and heart ache when I go to bed at night. Then the first thing in the morning, before breakfast, I start with two hours' piano practice of those everlasting scales, that Monsieur Gardier calls 'brilliant runs.' I know I should greatly prefer a run somewhere else. Then, after breakfast, one hour at French and German exercises—oh that horrid German grammar !—and Markham's *France*, afterwards natural history, *Magnall's Historical Questions*, then *Butler's Arithmetical Questions*, then singing lessons with that miserable little red-faced oddity, Signor Paletsky, who sticks up a mirror on the piano, and I have to adjust my mouth exactly to his fancy, and try to smile as I gasp out those horrid *do, re, mi, fa, sol, la, si, do's,* until I am absolutely ready to faint; then, in the afternoon, Latin exercises, the globes, and twice a week dancing and modern cookery—so you see, dear Sissy, how I am bothered. But I prefer even all this rather than be a cross old lady; for I do love kind words, and I do love to come to you, Sissy, you are so gentle—you never scold; but lately you have got a little dismal, and whenever I ask dear mamma why you don't come downstairs like you used, and do your pretty wool work, crochet, sing, play your guitar, and gather sweet flowers for the tiny vases in the rooms, she says, because you are upstairs ' moping.' I asked what she meant, and she replied, nothing particular. Now, Sissy dear, tell me something about moping."

"Alas! I know too well, dear one, to what

your mother refers; and to impart to you all the dismals that have created the 'mopping' to which she alludes, would be an act of indiscretion on my part, and would be only filling your young mind with bubbles, empty bubbles, and vanity."

"But you know mamma says I am a woman in reality, though not in years."

"God forbid, child, that you should be. Your young days, like the wildflowers in the hedgerows, will soon die away; the bloom of your youth will pass fast enough, and the thorns as well as the roses will spring up in clusters around you; the beautiful sunshine, the bright morning of your life, will swiftly fly, and the night with its dark mantle will—"

"Oh you dismal Sissy!" interrupted Gertrude, "you are getting like all the grown-up ladies, only you don't look angry, and you don't scold one bit. I wish you would, sometimes."

"I could not find the heart to scold you, dear," interposed Nora, smoothing her hand down her sister's wealth of hair.

"Not if I deserved it?—why?"

"I could not bear to see such a pretty face in trouble," said Nora, affectionately kissing her sister on both cheeks.

"Sissy, dear," said Gertrude, "you remember when we went into North Wales, to that beautiful estate belonging to Lady someone, do you not? You know when we stopped at the private hotel by the name of Pwllycrochon (or some such name), in Colwyn?"

"Yes, dear; or, as papa jocosely called it, 'Put-the-clock-on.'"

"And you remember we all went by rail to Bangor, don't you?" continued Gertrude.

"Perfectly well, dear."

"And you recollect we saw—oh, such a wonderful bridge; they called it the Menai, I think?"

" Yes, you are correct," rejoined Nora.

" The bridge was not so high, or nearly as Clifton Bridge, at St Vincent's Rocks, but it was longer, I think."

" Very much so," replied Nora thoughtfully, at the same time wondering at the child's curious detail.

" And we had a carriage and four horses, and a tipsy postillion, if you remember, and we drove to the foot of a wonderfully high mountain, that went up ever so far into the clouds ; am I right ? "

" We did," replied Nora abstractedly, " and most thoroughly enjoyed our visit. The scenery was beautiful, and the air supremely invigorating."

" And we were so happy, were we not, Sissy ? " rejoined Gertrude.

" Yes, love, as happy as doves."

There was a long pause at the end of this colloquy, during which time Gertrude was making an attempt at biting the back of one of her nails, a habit which was not usually hers ; then she continued, archly,—

"Do you remember, Sissy, the name of that lofty mountain—the highest, I believe, in England and Wales ?"

"Very well indeed, Gerty, it was Sno—"

A shudder ran through the frame of Nora. She saw in a moment that her sister had ingeniously led up to her own name!

"Don't stare so, Sissy, or look so wild !" exclaimed Gertrude ; "I know all about it, Mrs Snowdon, all about it."

"You know all about it ?"

"Dear me, yes, everyone in the castle, servants and all, are aware that you are married, and that you are a widow."

"The ice is broken, then," rejoined Nora. "God be praised, a weight is removed from my brain. Go, child, go downstairs and leave me ; I wish to be alone."

"One more kiss, Sissy," said Gertrude, "one more—and another. I shall come to-morrow, shall I not? I do love you so. I have a half holiday, let us spend it together at the waterfall in Barley Wood, all amongst the beautiful ferns we are so fond of."

"Yes, dear Gerty, if we are spared to see the morning, and we are well, we will go to-gether, and enjoy the amenity of the wild-flowers in the valley and coppice: the place you name is my favourite retreat."

"Call me early, won't you, dear Sissy? don't forget. Mamma says I am in reality a little woman!"

The door closed, and all was still except the sound of the receding steps of the light-hearted girl as she tripped through the corridor humming a lively tune.

"If one bright gleam of happiness has been torn from me," soliloquised Nora, "there are evidences of God's infinite goodness portrayed in that child, who comes, as it were, as a physician to bind up a broken heart, to administer to my sick mind some mild restorative. She possesses a charm which has a powerful antidote for allaying grief. The girl, of all others, who, I thought, would have nursed in her breast bitter feelings, and opposed me, now comes to my rescue, charged with the milk of human kindness, and, as it were, imparts new life.

Thoroughly worn with anxiety and brooding over the past, present, and the future, Nora sought the repose she so much needed; but her mind was restless, the counteraction of events brought her brain into more active play, thus driving sleep from her weary eyes.

As the clock in the old tower of Carthewin Castle struck the midnight hour, and the whole of the inmates were supposed to have forgotten, for a brief season, the things of this life, Nora's bedroom door was gently opened.

" Who's there ? "

No answer.

A fairy-like form glided into the room— a whisper—a kiss—a question—an answer —a gentle hand turned back the bedclothes, and Nora and Gertrude nestle in each other's arms until the faint streak of early dawn forced its way through the lattice casement, and the plaint of the cuckoo was heard in the distance.

CHAPTER XI.

TWO ROSES.

*" In youth how wide the field of hope—in age
how narrow ! "*

IT is in the middle of July, the sky is filled
with ultramarine blue, scarcely a flying scud
is to be seen; the lark, poised high in mid-
air, sings joyously; every living thing is
breathing the sweetness of the fields: the
green wheat - stalks are growing higher,
stronger, and waving majestically to the soft
breeze of a summer's morning, and the bright
poppies stand up here and there in the
furrows in gorgeous bloom. The balmy odour
from the broad beans, honeysuckle, and clematis perfume the air with ambrosial scents;

the wild rose, the traditional little friend, attracts the traveller's attention, as the queen of the lane with her host of off-shoots and tiny buds peep out invitingly from sweet briar branchlets and, as it were, tell of their joyous spring days of old. The bees are industriously plying their vocation as they vigorously search flower - cup, blossom, and leaf for maliferous food; many are returning loaded with pollen, homeward bound. Those rascally poachers, the crows, are cawing and swarming on the arable land, ploughing up with destructive beaks the soil, whilst others are perched high on the top of surrounding trees keeping watch—how different are the habits of the rooks! The mill-stream flows slowly and silently on until it reaches the ponderous machine whose motive power grinds the corn and cuts the timber for Carthewin Castle and estate; the monotonous sounds of the huge wheel moving round in

solemn like motion, and the dropping of the
water as it is carried over on its shiny verdant
surface, fills one with reminiscences of old,—
days of our childhood, the bright and happy
time of our youth, when the toy boat—that
traditional little galley—was gaily sailed on
the mill-stream,—the thatched cottage, the
dun cow with the crumpled horn, the apple-
faced dairy-maid, the miller all in white, the
old impromptu rustic bridge, the stile at the
bottom of the orchard, the deep well in the
yard, with its large coil of chain,—

> " The old oaken bucket,
> The iron-bound bucket,
> The moss-covered bucket,
> That stood by the well,"—

the small fishery of our childhood, with
withy stick, cork, thread, crooked pin and
worm,—the old mountain roan shaggy pony,
that once used to catch in the meadow by
coaxing with bread, saddling with various

shifts, and tally-hoing in the rear of the stream of hunters, sometimes creeping where best hunters could not jump,—the spills, the laughter, the return home with torn and dirty clothes,—the fun in the home orchard with Carlow, our favourite spaniel,—that bonny brown loaf and strawberry jam, with best of appetites,—the vigorous pull at the jug of new milk,—the fun in our bedrooms,— the war with pillows and bolsters,—the twelve hours' sleep,—the morning bath,—the rosy cheeks,—the bat, ball, fife, drum, and renewed peals of laughter round the hawthorn tree; are all pleasant recollections for those who have a soul for the memory of days long gone by. It may be so with some of my readers, as it is with the author, melodies of old singing within, an undying sweet song of early days, and all the light-hearted, joyous surroundings ever rising to the surface. In the words of Moore—

" You may break—you may ruin the vase if you will,
   But the scent of the roses will hang around it still."

Yes; all is peaceful as a summer's dream. The longest day has scarcely passed—there is but little night; and, when the dew begins to fall, it bathes with refreshing breath the thirsty flowers; the balmy odour fills the air with delicious scents.

" Summer, O sweet summer !
   How I love thy sunny hours ! "

.   .   .   .

There were some beautiful roses peeping in at the window of Carthewin Castle, and there were two roses peeping out—one in bloom and one in bud. Let us step inside and enjoy their fragrance.

Our heroine is engaged in "filling in" some wool work. Gertrude is seated on a small footstool by her side, looking very picturesque, reading aloud an interesting tale out of the monthly magazine. How lovely those twain looked ; how fond, too, they were growing of each other. Nora's sad bereavement brought her step - sister's fountain of love and sympathy into play. It flowed copiously, and, like a shower of pure water, invigorated the drooping bloom, and refreshed the leaves.

"Gerty, love," said Nora, parting the wealth of her sister's flowing hair, and kissing the back of her neck, "don't read any more of that tale."

"Oh, do let me, Sissy," replied Gertrude ; "it is so pretty. We have not got into the best of it yet, and I am so anxious to know what became of little Alice, and whether Clara marries Podmore, and whether that horrid old Dapper is hanged, and—"

"Never mind, pet, oblige me by not reading it. I will go to the library and bring you something infinitely more amusing, and much more instructive."

"I daresay, Sissy, dear, some cold, rusty, dismal thing or other. Papa is always boring me about travels and improving my mind. Why, I have read almost every book of travel in the library."

"Well, Gerty, travels, as a rule, are anything but dry; on the contrary, most amusing, and the best of them very instructive. You have not yet read *Central Europe*, or Dr Barth's *Central Africa*, or Washington Irving's *Columbus*, or—"

"Oh, yes; go on, Sissy. I expect you will conclude with Gibbon's *Decline and Fall of the Roman Empire*," interrupted Gertrude. "Now, I don't object to reading a life amongst the Indians. I think it is splendid to follow the customs and habits of the 'braves,' their old squaws and woolly-headed children; but why, Nora, don't you like me to finish this tale? Harry Podmore is such a nice, noble character, and old Dapper is such a horrid, nasty thing, that—"

"Notwithstanding, dear one," interrupted Nora, "I would rather you did not read aloud that book. It is not the best in the library for young minds ; indeed, there is much in it objectionable, and you can spend far sounder hours in possessing yourself of good material, instead of sowing the seed of those trashy novels. Bacon says, 'Reading makes a full man, writing, a correct one, and speaking, a ready man.'"

"Ah, now I have it!" said Gertrude, with a little toss of her head. "You are at your naughty tricks again,—those horrid dismals. I don't wonder at papa saying that he will send you to Uncle George at Cadiz, where you will mix with some lively ladies. I say, Nora, that reminds me, do you know mamma said this morning that we are going to have a swell garden-party?

The 'best people' are coming, and there is to be a wind-up in the large ballroom in the evening. It is to be an awfully grand affair, most *recherché!* All the Branscombs and the Winkworth girls are coming; also old Sir Robert Simens and the pretty girl—what's her name? who was not to be found on the memorable morning of the proposed wedding — the little wretch! I wonder at mamma having any desire to receive her after so much gossip; but mamma says she is so 'strictly county,' that it must be looked over. Now, tell me, what will you wear, Sissy ?"

" Such things seldom enter my head," replied Nora, with a weary sigh.

" Well, I never!" exclaimed Gertrude. " You are certainly what my governess calls an imperturbable being."

" I care but little for these ' swell' entertainments, as you call them, neither have I ever had an inclination to mingle in the vortex of frivolous society, Gerty."

" Anyhow, Sissy, I like a bit of fun," replied Gertrude, " and I like to be able to hold my own in the way of a little finery 'tip-top,' as Cousin Cuthbert says ; and, to that end, Messrs Robeall, of Regent Street, are to make me, oh, such a lovely dress ! with ever so many flounces, and it is to be looped up in festoons of I don't know what, so no more short dresses for me, Nora. Hurrah ! what fun it will be ; won't it ? "

" Tell me, Sissy, how old were you last birthday ? " said Nora, a little reproachfully.

" Last birthday ?—why, fifteen—that is, I am going in sixteen, don't you know ? "

" Ah, my child, there is ample time yet ; your mother had better keep you a child as long as she can. Nature, in all its rapid, certain course, will press back the springtide of your life fast enough without the aid of Messrs

Robcall, or consulting any artificial means for the purpose of making you look older than you really are."

" But you know, Sissy dear, as I told you before, mamma says, though I am a child in years, I am really a woman in manner ; and you know papa calls me his ' little old woman.' Upon my word, you are a naughty Nora. I do believe, had you the power, you would place me in a kind of Chinese slipper, so that I shouldn't grow one bit."

" No, Gerty, I would do nothing of the kind. I would rather see you grow day by day into more and more usefulness, and watch your youthful intellect expanding and ripening, but not unnaturally forced ; for do we not know that hothouse plants, cultured under the blaze of a scorching noonday's sun, pushed forward at night by artificial means, and denied the dew breath of heaven, are always tender plants."

"I think I shall give you a new name, Nora, — say Mrs Dismals, instead of Mrs Moping, as mamma calls you; for you are everlastingly comparing me in some way or other to flowers! If you could transmogrify me at this moment, what on earth would you convert me into?"

A long pause.

"I am not particular, Sissy," went on Gertrude, pursing up her pretty little mouth very considerably; "though it is well to remind you that I detest dandelions, and I should object to sweet peas and John Quills —I get too much of them already with Miss Reignforth—and none of your Tom Thumbs, for I want to grow to something tall. Now, Sissy, out with it, dear, and I have no doubt I shall be in the vase as a decoration for the dinner-table before I can say 'Please, don't!'"

"That will do, Gerty, I have hit upon it. I change you instantly into a scarlet-runner," said Nora jocosely; "and now run into the garden as fast as you can, and don't stop running until you have climbed up the green knoll at the top of the hill, that is covered with the mountain herbage."

"Dear Sissy, dear Mrs Mopings, I shall soon get you out of your dismals, I hope; why, you have positively laughed this morning. Nothing very crescendo though, as my professor of *do, re, mi* would say," and snatching up her garden hat, Gertrude opened the French window, bounded over the closely-shaven lawn, paused in the distance, kissed her hand again at her stepsister, waved her snow-white handkerchief, and the little light-hearted "scarlet runner" soon climbed out of sight.

The play of Gertrude's intellect was precisely what was wanted: the child seemed intuitively to know the exact antidote her sorrowing sister and her only close companion in life required ; her innocent ways and playful manner cheered and comforted the mourner when every other method failed. In the words of the poet Moore,—

" Earth has no sorrows that Heaven cannot heal."

" I love that child," said Nora, within herself; " what should I do without her? She is sent, as it were, like an angel from heaven, to cheer me in my lonely widowhood," and burying her face in her hands, she shed tears of gratitude, and softly murmured,—" Percy, my beloved Percy, I shall—"

" Soon be on board the *Bucephalus*, bound for Cadiz," said Mr Townsend, who approached unobserved.

" Oh dear ! how you frightened me, papa !" exclaimed Nora, placing her trembling hand upon her heart.

" Well, my daughter, what is it all about now ? " said Mr Townsend, pulling both ends of his whiskers, his habit when things did not please him.

" Nothing, papa," thoughtfully.

" Nothing, papa ! " repeated Mr Townsend, in a mimicking tone; " absurd ! I know better than that. Now, none of your old tricks, if you please, Nora, or, as sure as fate, I will have your boxes packed, and send you and—" A pause.

" Who ? " ventured Nora inquiringly.

" Your mamma to Cadiz, for change of air," continued Mr Townsend significantly.

" You could not be so unkind, I know," said Nora, throwing up her soft eyes, which were suffused with tears, into her father's face, and resting her hand on his manly shoulder.

" I think it would be an act of kindness," ventured Mr Townsend.

" Say rather one of cruelty," responded Nora, with a sob in her throat. " God forgive me for using such a term, papa. I know right well, from past experience, that cruelty forms no part of your nature."

Mr Townsend flamed crimson, but it instantly faded away, as he continued,—

"I will not adopt any course, my dear daughter, or force a thing upon you, unless it meet with your approval. At the most, Nora, I can have but a few years to live, and I should like to spend the residue of them in something like tranquillity; without that peace, life becomes a burden. I lay myself out in every possible way, shape, and form, for the benefit of my wife and you girls. My hopes are built in you, and no pleasure is so great to me, or lasting, as to see you all pulling together in the most united way, in harmony and happiness. The trial that you have passed through, my daughter, the effects of which you are manifestly still suffering from, has been a crushing one, and it is fortunate for you that things are no worse. Sympathy, I fear, will avail but little, else I would hasten to the rescue, and try to help you out of the difficulty. As the scythe clears the meadow of the long grass, or the hook the thistle in the hedge-row, so will time in its season clear your brow of the dark clouds that hover over it."

" Never ; never entirely ! " said Nora.

"Tush, child! tush ! you offer an in-dignity to your heavenly Father by nursing such wild thoughts, and giving way to desponding imagination."

The moving pathos of Mr Townsend's words greatly affected our heroine, as she said,—

" Dear papa, how I love to be with you, and feel the warmth of your sunny smile."

" Now, Nora dear, throw off all dismals, and go to the library and sit with your mamma for an hour or so. I know, from what she said this morning, she wishes to see you."

" Oh, papa, please don't, I—I—"

" It is my desire," said Mr Townsend, drawing himself up impressively, with a lofty air.

" I am ever obedient, father, to your commands, but you know nothing of my trouble."

" Pish ! what absurdity ! it cannot possibly be a Townsend who is talking such nonsense. Think of your lamented mother's moral and intellectual excellence, and what she would have said to you had she been spared. Come, come, no more of this, child ; no more ; go, now, and sit awhile with Mrs Townsend ; put your first foot foremost, the best side, so to speak, towards London ; brace up your nerves ; be watchful over your words ; recollect, love, to whom you will be speaking,—my wife !—your step-mother ! be humble, as you have need to be, after what has transpired ; but with becoming pride stand fast to the traditions of your family ; and, above all things, lose sight of the fact that you are the heiress of Carthewin. For the future, Nora, I rely upon you with the most absolute confidence ; I obliterate the past from my memory ; I anticipate that which is before us with all the fervour of a devoted parent, and I shall look for, as a natural result, a reciprocation on your part."

"I feel, dear father, that I am wholly unworthy of so much thought and consideration ; you have chosen, however, in your paternal love to deal gently with me—yes, with astounding forbearance — and my sweet sister, that lily of the vale, that cherub of the spring, is something worth living for. And you, oh, my dear father, so long as there is left a caressing tendril to my frail nature, it will cling to thee !"

" If there be one thing more than another I am rejoiced at, my daughter, it is seeing Gertrude and you growing up together in perfect harmony, bearing with one another, and loving one another with all earnestness and purity of your fond nature."

" Do you wish me to go to Uncle George's at Cadiz, father ?" said Nora, with the sweet-est expression.

" Cadiz be hanged ! Not I, child. Throw off all your dismals, and I can devise plans whereby your happiness, and my happiness, and all our happiness will, with God's bless-ing, be complete."

" Mamma will be kind to me, won't she ?"

" Kind, child ! of course, she will. Do you think for one moment I should allow her to be otherwise ? God forbid ! Besides, she is so good and considerate ; I am sure my pretty blue eyes," continued Mr Townsend, pressing his daughter's chiselled face with both hands, " she loves you, and she will, if you mind your p's and q's, be devoted to you."

Those p's and q's ! !

"Thank you very much, dear father," said our heroine, pinking considerably, whilst the flash of her eyes and subdued pout of her coral lips showed some little signs of tumult within. " I will strenuously endeavour to take very considerable care of those letters of warning, if only for your dear sake," and Nora struggled with emotion.

" Heaven bless you, my daughter," responded Mr Townsend, turning his head suddenly away to avoid exposing tears that had quickly gathered in his eyes.

And then followed the heavy step of the lord of the manor, as he walked up the highly-polished oak staircase to his dressing-room.

CHAPTER XII.

PAST, PRESENT, AND FUTURE.

On the morning of the last day of July there were assembled in the old oak room of Carthewin Castle, Mrs Townsend, Nora, and Gertrude. The former was seated at her secretaire, busily engaged in replying to numerous letters which had accumulated through slight indisposition. A keen observer could have detected that the lady of the house, as she paused now and again in her correspondence, and gazed abstractedly through the open French window on the closely-shaven lawn, looked somewhat worn and anxious; the slight rubicund tinge that usually prevailed on either cheek had

vanished, leaving her a complexion sallow
and suggestive of much gastric derangement,
contrasting immensely with her large dark
lustrous hazel eyes, and the ample folds of
black tresses, which were wreathed in various
devices around a well-moulded head. The
point of a tiny purple satin slipper peeped
from the skirt of a cream-coloured morning
dress; the little foot at intervals seemed
greatly agitated, by tattooing the floor whenever its wearer's eyes wandered from the
letter she was writing, to Nora, and from
Nora to Gertrude.

Some beautiful roses were peeping in at
the window, their offshoots gracefully bending to and fro at every slight breeze, carrying with it sweet, balmy odours of honeysuckle, clematis, and other summer scents.

Nora is looking very picturesque, more
cheerful and animated; and although her
bright fresh colour has not re-appeared,

nevertheless, from constant exposure to the sun, and her wild rambles in all kinds of weather over her father's domain, her skin has become much bronzed, and a superficial observer would arrive at the conclusion that she was brimful of health, without even a semblance of care or anxiety. Her fairly tall and graceful figure, as she silently moved about the polished floor decorating the tiny vases with the choicest of hot-house flowers, greatly resembled the full-sized portrait of her late mother, which hung in the oak room.

Placid she sits in her picture,
  Reposing in velvet arm-chair ;
Her form stands out on the canvas,
  Whilst her soul is heaven knows where.

Pensive and silent she watches
  Loved ones that are flitting so near,
Breath, as it were, of her spirit,
  Breathes softly on all that is dear.

Gentle the sigh that's uplifted,
  And wafted with swift wings above ;
Tender the throes of a fond heart,
  And throbbings of exquisite love.

Sweetly she smiles on her offspring,
    Her brow is divested of care ;
Angels are now her companions,
    Some here, there, and everywhere.

Calmly she sits in her picture,
    Her half-parting lips seem to speak,
Her eyes with tears are o'erflowing,
    A bright pink suffuses her cheek.

'Tis not the outcome of sadness,
    But rather the voice of the dead
Whispering of love and affection,
    And warnings of breakers ahead !

No one could look on that portrait, and then on the stately form of our heroine, without being struck with the close resemblance to the mother and child; the finely formed head ; the sweet frank eyes ; the rosebud mouth ; the well-defined Grecian nose ; the dimpled chin, and sloping shoulders, are portrayed in every line of the shadow and substance.

Rarely a night passed without Nora crept quietly into the old oak room, and gazed, unobserved, on her beloved mother's portrait :

though an infant in arms when her parent died, nevertheless there was an irresistible attraction to that room and its surroundings. Our heroine never felt happier than when she could find an opportunity to procure her late mother's portfolio, in which could be found some valuable and touching memoirs of her life. Unfortunately for Nora, she possessed a painfully sensitive disposition, and felt keenly the effect of any observation which had the slightest taint of unkindness, whether its arrow were directed towards her, or any of her family or friends. During the whole period of her life, that most excellent trait in her character earned for herself the highest esteem of all her circle of acquaintance.

Gertrude is of a somewhat different stamp. She is now fifteen years old, tall, sprightly, a perfect blonde, with a warm, rich colouring, which lit up the sweetest of eyes. Though her forehead is low, it is broad—gentleness and sympathy can be read on her brow. She is as joyous as the lark, and as innocent as the lamb careering in the home park. Her lithe rounded form, superb neck and arms, filled one with rapture at every turn she took ; her merry laugh, which rang out peals of gladness in the hall of Carthewin Castle, spoke its own sweet language of her young, bright, happy life,—her spring-tide flowing gently into womanhood, like a beautiful flagrant flower unfolding its leaves day by day. Truly it may be said that she blossomed brightly beneath her father and mother's fostering care. Her unbounded love for her step-sister, which was reciprocated by Nora with all the tenderness of her fond nature, her touching child-like ways and playful disposition, were most attractive.

Mrs Townsend threw down her long quill pen with some determination, sealed her last letter with apparent haste, closed the secretaire, one thought a little violently, saying,—

" There, dear girls, I have now finished all my arrears of correspondence ; if I had to consult my own feelings in the matter, I should not write another letter for the next three months," and, with a very dignified air, she walked across the room to Gertrude, continuing, " My love, I want you to take this letter over to the rectory—the walk will do you good—and if the Reverend Mr Branscomb and Lady Branscomb are at home, deliver it yourself, and wait for an answer."

" With all pleasure, mamma," replied Gertrude, turning the letter over musingly.

" Well, what now ? " said Mrs Townsend. " You are an inquisitive little puss. If the truth were known, you are anxious to learn the contents."

" I partly guess, mamma, for I heard you talking with papa at the breakfast - table yesterday; is it not an invitation for the Branscombs to dine here on Friday?"

"Yes, my pet, you are right for once. Nora, love, you have not promised to go anywhere on that day, I hope?"

"I have not made any engagement," replied Nora, pinking slightly; "neither should I think of doing so, without consulting you, mamma."

"If you had consulted me, Nora, in another matter at an early stage, I might have rescued you from the very distressing ordeal you have had to pass through," replied Mrs Townsend, somewhat cynically.

Nora held down her head; the colour crimsoned her cheeks to her very ears; she felt the home-thrust; a deep sigh and a glistening tear on the longest of lashes, told its own tale of sadness, and the chaotic tumult that was wrestling within. There was a manifest tone of mockery in Mrs Townsend's remarks, but our heroine concealed to the utmost her agitation, as she tremblingly replied,—

" I sincerely hope that you will not again refer to my clandestine marriage. Heaven only knows what I have suffered, and how much I am now enduring, on account of my precipitation."

" Fiddlesticks ! " interrupted Mrs Townsend.

" The act," continued Nora, " was mine own ; the crushing blow has fallen on my head, and affects me only."

" I am not quite so sure of that," said Mrs Townsend sarcastically.

" I fail to see," continued Nora, " that it seriously concerns any other person than my father, to whom I have made every possible reparation for an act of indiscretion."

" Indeed ! that may be your view, Nora, but I beg most emphatically to state that it is not mine ; and I consider your observations but a very poor return for the anxious days and nights I have endured on your behalf since I took up my abode in this dreary castle, and watched over you in your tender years with a maternal love—your own lamented mother could not have done more."

"I am very sensible of the obligation I owe to your kind favour," replied Nora, somewhat discomposed, "and I trust that Providence will permit me to return to you and yours, those acts of kindness and duty that my extreme youth and your position with my father rendered almost imperative for you to pursue."

At the word "imperative," Mrs Townsend visibly flushed, and fussily crossed and re-crossed the room, with somewhat mixed feelings of pleasure and grief—pleasure, because she felt pleased at the manifestations of obligation—and grief, because she seemed to regret that Nora should have touched upon a moral duty which she well knew was hers, from the very hour she became the wife of Godfrey Townsend, and which duty, she was well aware, had been to a certain extent neglected.

After the birth of Gertrude, almost the entire conduct of our heroine (as before stated) devolved upon the Honourable Mrs Mackenzie, whose antecedents were of the very highest order, and it is due to that lady to place upon record that she most religiously discharged the duties entrusted to her; but there was one vital thing wanting — a mother's fostering care, a parent who could take the child at intervals from her studies, and mould her little heart and brain, teaching her (as only a parent can teach) the way she should go, instilling into her youthful mind the lights and shades of the world, with all its bright and best influences, as well as its allurements, disappointments, and vanities.

"My dear Nora," said Mrs Townsend, with a voice gentle in its accents, and aspiring to tears, then drawing her chair in close proximity to her step-daughter's, continued, "I have an exposed nerve, and you have touched it. Come, dear child, we will hope and endeavour to be better friends for the future. Upon second consideration, I sometimes think it would have been infinitely preferable, in the interest of your future advancement in life, if I had not left you so much to the care and discipline of the Honourable Mrs Mackenzie, whose aptitude for—"

"Mamma, suffer me to interrupt you; I cannot allow anyone, directly or indirectly, to cast the slightest reflection on my late governess for any shortcomings of my own; she is not here to defend herself, but, happily,

I know how to value the past devoted services of that good and pious lady. I look
back over years of my childhood with the
fondest remembrance of her inestimable
worth. I can never feel too grateful for
the sound hours she spent in the hope of
training her little Nora (as she called me)
to the standard of her own moral excellence. Were I to feel otherwise, I should
not only be unworthy of the position I
hold in her kind, loving heart, but I should
forfeit her esteem."

Mrs Townsend was a lady of unaccountable
impulse, with a countenance that one could
not easily decipher : love and hatred, likes
and dislikes, warmth and coldness, under-
went swift changes ; devoted to her husband,
and passionately attached to her own daughter, in whom all her hopes were centred ;
but from the hour she became the consort
of Godfrey Townsend—

"If the veil from the heart could be torn,
    Or the mind could be read on the brow,"

we should discover that there was a want
of love and devotion which, to all right-
thinking women, should have existed for
the motherless child she promised her husband to protect, and it should have formed,
as it were, a part of her marriage contract.

The *frou-frou* of Mrs Townsend's ample
dress, as she hurriedly left the room, passing through the French casement to the
lawn, was suggestive of some displeasure
at the eulogistic terms used by Nora in
favour of her late governess. May be it
was the outcome of the light and shade
that she thought was portrayed in the
weakness of her own past actions and the
strength of the Honourable Mrs Mackenzie.
Anyhow, the observation that emanated
from Nora jarred very considerably on Mrs
Townsend's sensitive ear, as she tremulously

requested the footman to order the carriage for the usual morning drive.

Nora inwardly felt that she may have unconsciously ventured too far, as she well knew that her late governess was never any favourite of her step-mother's. She could well recollect, when first entering her "teens," and for many subsequent years, the numerous trifling disputes that arose from time to time between her father and Mrs Townsend, relative to the Honourable Mrs Mackenzie's profound attachment to her. She had often been a witness to words spoken in anger on behalf of herself, the remembrance of which rushed with mighty force to her memory as she followed her step-mother to the conservatory, and, placing her arm round her waist, said, with her sweetest expression,—

"I hope I have not vexed you, dear mamma!"

"Vexed me, child!" replied Mrs Townsend, in low, sympathetic tones, and carelessly picking some dead leaves from a plant.

"I fear I may, unknowingly, have said something offensive to you," said Nora. "If I have, oh, bear with me, forgive me, my heart is so full!"

(*To be continued.*)

END OF VOL. I.

www.ingramcontent.com/pod-product-compliance
Lightning Source LLC
Chambersburg PA
CBHW021043030726
47496CB00006B/1669